Zombie Girl 2 Infection

Copyright © 2017 by Elle Klass
ISBN - 978-0-9982709-8-2
Published by Books by Elle, Inc.
Cover art created by TL Katt
Editor Dawn Lewis Bookmarks Editing
For more information go to
http://elleklass.weebly.com/
Blog: http://thetroubledoyster.blogspot.com
Facebook:
https://www.facebook.com/ElleKlass
Twitter- @elleklass

Author's Disclaimer

This story is entirely fictional. No one was actually hurt, zombie or not, in the making of this book. Any characters, places or events are purely figments of the author's imagination. No part of this publication may be reproduced, transmitted or redistributed either in its entirety or in part without the author's express written consent.

Books in the Zombie Girl Series

Premonition
Infection
Retribution - coming soon

Other Books by Elle

As Snow Falls

Bloodseeker Series
The Vampires next Door
The Monster Upstairs

Baby Girl Series
In the Beginning Book I
Moonlighting in Paris Book II
City by the Bay Book III
Bite the Big Apple Book IV
Caribbean Heat BookV
Baby Girl Box Set -Books I - IV

The Ruthless Storm Trilogy
Eye of the Storm Eilida's Tragedy
The Calm Before the Storm Evan's Sins
In the Midst of the Storm Tommy's Deception

1

Chapter One

After we picked my dad up from the hospital we stopped at Sonic and grabbed burgers. It was late and Mom didn't feel like cooking. I picked at my tots on the way home and managed to eat about half my *Chili Cheese Coney*. My stomach gurgled and rolled as I thought about Bryce. He definitely recognized me, and I tried to think of any excuse to go back into the hospital, but my dad was tired and sore, luckily not injured seriously, but ready to get home. I couldn't make him wait for me. Bryce's touch was real. He was real. *Did we share a dream?* I'd gone back and forth with the premonition idea. Today confirmed it *or did my course of action modify the sequence of history?* My thinking was crazy, but Bryce and I shared the premonition --- the recognition in his eyes told me. I was sure the zombie-takeover apocalypse was near. I felt it in every pore of my skin, and in my bones.

I went to bed early, locking my door in case tonight was the night. In my dream, I'd gone to bed without dinner after getting chewed out by my parents for my F in science. They made me leave my phone with them. Today probably wasn't the day, but it was better to be safe than sorry. *Do premonitions always happen as seen?* I wasn't sure, so I Snapchatted Sarah to hear her voice and see her face.

She answered with a huge smile. Her tight curls sprang everywhere. "Hey."

"Hey," I responded, and then told her about my dad's accident and seeing Bryce at the hospital. The moment he brushed past me and we touched made the entire dream a reality -- finding him behind the crate, stuffing the metal object into the brainstems of the zombies and Bryce and I making it to Earnest Earl, my dad's boat.

"Maddie, do you know what this means?" she asked with an edge of excitement.

"It means my dream really was a premonition and the zombie apocalypse is happening soon," I answered hypothetically.

"Maddie, off the phone," hollered my mom from her bedroom across the hall. I really needed to talk with Sarah but it would have to wait until morning.

With hesitation I said, "I gotta go, see you tomorrow."

I checked my window, making sure it was locked tight, then stuffed my phone beneath my pillow and drifted off to sleep. A tapping at my window woke me. My heart beat like a marching band as I twisted my head towards the window. The curtains were drawn, but I saw the distinct outline and shadow of someone on the other side.

I shuddered involuntarily then eased out of bed and stalked towards the window. The shadow hadn't moved. It tapped again. *What if it's a zombie? They don't tap and wait. Get a grip!* I told myself, but it didn't make me feel any better. I clenched my fists together. Realizing my hands were empty, I scanned my room for a convenient weapon. The lamp on my

3

dresser was the closest thing, so I grabbed it. It yanked back at me and I fell sideways towards my dresser. *You gotta unplug it dummy!* I said inside my head, then pulled the cord from the wall. Taking a deep breath, I moved the curtains aside and peeked out. I sighed relief and my heartbeat returned to normal when I saw it was Bryce kneeling below the window. He smiled when he saw my face. At least he wasn't a zombie. I undid the lock and slid the window open.

Through the screen I asked, "Bryce?" His hair was still tied back in a neat ponytail unlike the haphazard one in the dream.

"You had the dream too?" he asked with wide eyes.

I nodded. "I don't get it," I stated, then my mind switched gears. *How did he find me?* We were never at my house in the dream. "How did you find me?"

His chestnut hair hung in waves touching his shoulders and the moonlight made his green eyes sparkle. He was better looking in person. "The compass." In the dream he'd given me the compass. Somehow I brought it out of the dream with me. "My uncle makes them. It looks old, but it's not. He just makes them that way. Inside is a GPS chip. I didn't think to check it until I saw you today and it led me here. Look," he said, holding up his phone. It displayed a map with a blinking green light in my room.

"That's kinda creepy and stalkerish," I said, wrinkling my nose.

He shrugged it off. "We need to talk. Can I come in?"

I thought about my parents and decided it would be safer for me to go outside. "I'll meet you by the back gate."

Within minutes, I'd quietly snuck down the hall and through the living room, glided the sliding glass door open and slipped outside. He waited by the gate like I asked, and I let him in and steered him to an area furthest from my parents' room to the back of the yard by a tall, bushy maple tree so they wouldn't hear us.

He shifted on his feet and his eyes soaked me in. "Um… I don't know what's happening or why, but something is going to happen."

I knew that. "People don't share dreams. Somehow we're connected. Like a spiritual link. It sounds insane but I haven't stopped thinking about it."

He shifted onto his other foot, then clumsily grabbed my hands, as if nervous either about touching me or saying what was on his mind. "This is going to sound crazier, but I think we're supposed to figure this out and prevent it."

I enjoyed the touch of his hands on mine. My silly crush on him started the moment he kissed me in the dream, since my mind wandered to that moment frequently. In fact, it distracted me, and I almost missed hearing what he said. All I got was 'figure it out and prevent it'. *How could we prevent something we didn't understand?* I glanced at him, his green eyes blazing into mine. *Did he know something?*

5

I narrowed my eyes. "What do you know?" This was definitely weird and awkward. We'd never actually met before yet were talking like we'd known each other for years or had gone on a zombie killing spree. Life and death fighting had a way of bringing people together.

He shook his head. "Nothing. It's an observation, and it's stupid."

I wanted to stomp my foot and roll my eyes, but controlled myself. If I wanted to wrench it out of him, I needed to be patient and gentle. "Nothing is stupid. We don't have a clue what we're dealing with, and the premonition didn't give us any ideas about how the apocalypse starts, so please tell me what's on your mind."

He heaved a breath. "The premonition?" he repeated, as if he'd never thought of it that way or didn't know what it was. I stared at him, my eyes blazing 'get on with it' into his. As if his brain heard me he began. "The mosquito population has been heavier than usual this year. I noticed it, but when I heard my dad talking about it over the phone, I realized it wasn't just me. He's an environmental scientist who works in water management, and it's his job to keep track of species populations and other environmental factors."

I thought about it. We lived in North Florida, mosquitoes lingered year around, especially during warm winters. It didn't get cold enough to kill them, and the past winter had been unseasonably warm. All winter, we had three nights when the temperature dropped below thirty-five degrees

Fahrenheit; usually we had a couple weeks. My news-watching confirmed our unusually high, record-breaking temperatures. Nobody complained, since most people lived in Florida to escape the cold.

"We also had a warm winter, so isn't it normal then to have more flying vampires?" That's what I called them, as I was highly allergic. When they bit me, I had to be given a shot immediately or I'd swell up like a watermelon. My mom bought me bug repellent nail polish to keep them away. It worked really well; so well they never bothered me and I forgot about them.

"Yeah, but that's weird too. The whole continent has suffered warmer weather and higher mosquito populations," his face was stoic as the words left his mouth.

I shrugged. "It's possible. Mosquitoes are known to carry diseases, the Zika virus and malaria," I mumbled off.

"Exactly, so maybe a virus has mutated or something."

I wondered what else his father talked about in his work conversation, *and what about lovebugs? Didn't they eat mosquitoes?* I'd been paying attention in science. If the mosquito population was up, then its natural predators, A.K.A. lovebugs, would be really bad this spring. "Doesn't that mean we're going to have a bad lovebug season?" I abhorred the nasty little black creatures with their orangey-red heads. They got their name because the male and female flew around attached while mating and died still attached. The creatures were a nuisance that love vehicles and paint. During the season, I had to wash their nasty, acidic juices off my parents' cars. I cringed at the thought of more of them.

He chuckled. "You believe that rumor?"

I didn't respond with words but body gestures, by crossing my arms over my chest and tensing my face. The "rumor" seemed like truth, or at least believable. According to various minds in Florida, lovebugs were made in a lab at the University of Florida.

His chuckle migrated into a full-fledged laugh. Between snorts he said, "That's an urban myth. They migrated from Central America."

I narrowed my eyes and stared him down. "So glad I amused you."

He sobered from his glee-high and surprised me as he grabbed my hands, pulling me towards him, then leaned in and kissed my cheek. Its heat burned into my face and sent ripples of passion across my spine.

"I gotta go before my dad knows I'm gone. He was in a fender bender earlier and took a couple sleeping pills, but I shouldn't chance it," he stated, dropping my hands and walking towards the gate, leaving me in a quandary.

Chapter Two

*A*ccident? *Was his dad in the same accident as mine? Is that what causes the zombie takeover?* I was paranoid. The warm sensations of his hands were replaced by a piece of paper. I unfolded it. Bryce left me his phone number, but so long as I had the compass it would lead him directly to me.

I called him. I know -- let the guy call first -- wait three days, yada, yada. We had a world to save before the population was lost to a virus or plague and might not have three days. He answered right away.

"Maddie, is everything OK?"

He'd only been gone a couple minutes; the zombies didn't take over the world in that short amount of time. "I'm fine. Save my number. We may need to contact each other in an emergency."

"You missed me."

The same smart aleck charm as in the dream. "Text me when you get home so I know you didn't get bit on the way. I don't need you to turn before I have the chance to go Zombie Girl crazy." Not that I knew a bite would do it, but it did in the movies and one had to consider all possibilities.

"OK."

I woke up at five a.m. with another growing dread lump in my gut. My parents were still asleep, so I snuck into the garage and rummaged through my mom's car, searching for the keys to Earnest

Earl. They were on the floor of my mother's car, exactly as they were in my dream. Goose pimples rippled across my arms. There wasn't time to linger on it as I sent Sarah and Bryce a text to meet up at the park near the high school.

Sarah met me in the patch of trees behind the portables; from there we walked to the park. Bryce waited for us, leaning against a beat up blue Mazda.

"What's going on?" he asked, looking sexy.

Sarah sucked in a deep breath as she checked him out, then glanced in my direction and fanned her face. It was our sign for hottie.

I gave Sarah an 'I told you so' smirk, then got straight to the point. Saving the world didn't allow us time to linger over trivial things like teen eye candy. "I got the keys to Earnest Earl. I think we should make a copy and stock up the boat."

They both stared at me. Sarah spoke first, "Tomorrow is Saturday. We can do it then."

"But what if we can't?" I thought of how my dream ended with waking up to a 'normal' Saturday morning in my house. Today was Friday and that is when the premonition apocalypse began. I folded my arms across my chest.

"You're suggesting we skip school. We're kids, people are going to notice if we're running around the city," said Bryce, folding one leg over the other.

I pleaded to both of them, giving them puppy eyes. It usually worked on my parents. "Please. I think we should do it today. We can't wait."

They agreed. Bryce was the oldest and a senior, so we sent him in to make the keys. After, we stopped at my house and collected water bottles, canned foods, and weapons. At Sarah's and Bryce's we collected more food and a few items useful as weapons. The fact that our parents worked made it easy to slip in and out, then make it to the boat.

We dumped everything into a pile to take inventory. For food, we had plenty of drinks, boxed and canned foods; enough to last us for several months. We stuffed the cabinets and piled food into the bedrooms. I checked the windows, remembering my bedroom window was open in the dream. To the lack of my surprise, it was open a tiny bit. I slid it shut and locked it, then checked the others.

When I returned to Sarah and Bryce they were completing weapon inventory. We had a couple bats, a couple knives, a fireplace poker, a heavy hammer, two flashlights and extra batteries, an ax, and an oversized wrench, along with a couple shovels. I surveyed everything. "That's not a bad collection. We'll have to get pretty close." I paused for a second. "We can knock them down with the bats then stab them in the head, or you can just lop their heads off with a shovel," I said, smiling at Bryce as I picked up a shovel and ran my fingers over the sharp edge.

"Eww!" said Sarah, wrinkling her nose.

"Meet Zombie Girl," Bryce said with a smirk.

I flashed him the eye.

"Zombie Girl?" She wrinkled her nose.

"She's a killing machine," he said, then climbed up the ladder and sat above us, his feet dangling over the side.

11

I shrugged and gazed up at Bryce. "We need to put all this away. Get down here and help us."

His eyes stared hard at something in the distance. He squinted them like he was studying hard.

I sighed and mumbled, "Whatever," under my breath then picked up the bats and shovels, stuffing them beneath the seats. They might come in handier outside the cabin then inside. "Sarah, can you hand me a flashlight?"

When she didn't respond, I turned to see she'd climbed up the ladder too. They were both staring at something beyond my line of sight. "What the heck?!"

Sarah stared down at me. "Get up here, something's going on!"

I sighed and joined them up top.

Bryce pointed. "Follow my arm, look beyond the tip of my middle finger."

Lovebugs flew past us; yuck, the season was starting. I swatted at them, then gazed beyond his arm, noting how firm and muscular it was. There was a mess of lights and cars surrounding a wreck or something. I didn't even know what road it was, but it looked like a main artery. I remembered my dad's binoculars and scrambled downstairs, grabbed them, then scrambled back up. It was definitely a wreck. My eye studied the ambulances, then saw paramedics loading a stretcher into the back.

"What do you see?" asked an anxious Sarah.

I passed them to her. She snatched them immediately, placing them to her eyes. "OMG! That's a nasty wreck!"

Car accidents weren't exactly news around here, but a huge one that backed up traffic might make the news.

"More cops just showed up. Look!" She passed the binoculars back to me.

We all stood in eighty-seven degrees, ninety percent humidity air, on the top of my dad's boat, baking from the inside out like a microwave meal. I grasped the binoculars and placed them against my eyes. Three more State Troopers showed up, lights blazing and sirens blaring. I read the side of their cars. It had to be the freeway, I-95 maybe.

I dropped the binoculars. "It's late. School's out, we need to get home."

Bryce grabbed the binoculars and Sarah stated, "Its Friday. No school tomorrow. Hello!"

I nodded. "But I want to get home before my parents." Sarah was right, but I felt that I needed to be home. *What if today was the day?*

Bryce dropped the binoculars. "I agree with Maddie. I need to check on my dad. Since the accident, he hasn't been good."

I understood what he meant. My dad had suffered joint pain since his accident. Today he went to work. The hospital cleared him and gave him a prescription of muscle relaxers. That reminded me. "There's a first aid kit on the boat, but that may not be enough. We need to collect medical supplies. Bryce, can you pick us up in the morning?"

We made a tentative plan on the way home. Bryce would pick us up in the morning and tonight we'd raid our parents' medicine chests and gather supplies. I knew my mom was a prescription whore. She never threw them away when we didn't use them all.

Chapter Three

The drive was slow going. I guessed they must have rerouted traffic because of the accident, stuffing the other roads with excess commuters, so I sent my mom a text that we'd gone with a friend to the mall after school.

When I walked into the house, my mom flashed me the evil eye.

I forced a toothy smile, hoping it looked natural. "Hi, Mom."

"Where have you been?" My father's voice boomed from the living room. My mom stared at me, arms folded over her chest and her toe tapping against the tile floor. It echoed inside my head.

"I texted you, Mom. It's Friday we went to the mall after school," I stated in my no big deal voice.

"Take a seat," my dad offered, his voice gentle.

Oh no, they were getting ready to grill me. I dropped my smile. My mom followed me into the living room. "I'm going to jump right to it, Maddie. You weren't in school today."

What? How did they know? "Sure I was," I countered.

"Then explain this message." She replayed a message from her cell phone. It was a recorded message, "Your child, Maddie Smyth, missed one or more classes in school today."

I grinned, then sighed, coming up with a response that rolled off my tongue so naturally it surprised me. "I was late for math today. Mr. Johnson must have forgotten to mark me present."

My mom dropped her arms and relaxed. "Maybe. I'll call and clear it up Monday, but for tonight you're staying in. No Sarah's. Late isn't as bad as skipping, but it's still not acceptable and you need to know that."

If only they knew… "No Sarah and no phone. Drop it on the table before you sulk off to your room," my dad ordered, his voice firm yet pleasant at the same time. He had a way of doing that.

My dream poured back into my head as I dropped my phone on the table. I changed the course of history, but only the small events. I wasn't in trouble for my science grade, but for tardiness. Monday, they'd know I actually was skipping. I let out a breath and stalked to my room, dragging my heels. I heard my mom join my father and the squish of the couch then their low voices as they talked, most likely about me.

The events were happening: my dad's keys; being in trouble; even the darn lovebugs were out. I remembered them in my dream, stuck in zombie blood on the windshield. It all ran through my mind as I fell backwards on my bed and stared at the ceiling.

After a couple hours, I strolled outside my room. I hadn't been sent to it, I just couldn't use my phone or see Sarah, so I decided I should act normal. For several months now, I'd been joining them in the evenings for TV when I was home.

Shock clutched me as I strolled into the hallway. Their eyes fixed on the TV. *An SUV crossed the median into oncoming traffic, injuring the driver and passengers of the other vehicle. The driver of the SUV was pronounced dead...* The voice drowned as I watched shaky video footage like someone took it from their cell phone. A covered body lying on a stretcher lifted upward, the coverings dropping from her face. Her legs fell to the side in stiff movements and she tumbled off the stretcher. Whatever pedestrian was shooting the footage zoomed in on her face. I recognized it and fear rushed over me like a tidal wave.

Her dark skin, a couple shades lighter and ashy. Her oval face solemn, with a straight, gray line replacing the vivacious smile she always wore, but her eyes were the most perplexing, usually a coffee brown, now dull and pallid. Her blouse hung haphazardly around her shoulders. *Sarah's mother! This was it. How Sarah turned into a zombie too!*

I gawked with my parents, almost positive this was the accident we'd seen earlier, anxiety filling me as I watched the footage. The camera operator zoomed out as Sarah's mother walked towards a paramedic, her movements rigid, but not as stiff as the zombies in my premonition. *Yes!* Everything was happening and so quickly all I could do was stare and mumble inside my head: *It's happening! It's really happening.*

My mom looked at me, her face solemn and a tear lingering in the corner of her eye. Sarah and I had been best friends since forever. She knew her mother well. "Maddie, are you alright?"

No, no I wasn't alright, but how do I tell them? It was too late for Sarah's mom but not her. Please not her and my parents. I could save them. How do I save them? "I—"

My phone ringing cut me off. We all stared at it as if it was a giant moose, swiping its feet at the ground as it readied itself to annihilate us.

I glanced toward them, meeting their gazes, my eyes shifting from one to the next. The phone was still on the hall table and close enough I saw the screen. It was Bryce. "I have to get this," I stated with a shaky voice, reaching for the phone. I wasn't going to wait for their response but they didn't fight it and probably thought it was Sarah.

Before he got a word out, mine tumbled out of my mouth. "It's happening. Sarah. We have to get her!"

"She's with me and we're on our way." The unmistakable sound of urgency in his voice.

"Is she OK?"

"For the most part. She saw…" He paused for a second. "There's more. Our ETA is ten minutes." The phone cut off.

I turned, my parents staring at me. Their eyes wide and wearing matching confused expressions.

There was no way to say 'the zombie apocalypse is here' without sounding ridiculous and insane. It wasn't the time to worry. I was going with Bryce and Sarah and, if I had to duct tape them and force them into the car, my parents were coming too! "Listen to me. There isn't any time. You saw it, same as me.

People are turning into zombies and we need to leave."

My mother turned down the TV volume and narrowed her eyes, but her voice was soft. "Honey, the paramedics messed up in pronouncing her dead. She wasn't."

"Yes, she was. Didn't you see what she looked like?!"

"Maddie, sit down. You're not going anywhere, and zombies aren't taking over the world," Dad said, the normal flushness of his cheeks gone, substituted with white and his eyes missing their normal shine.

"Do you feel OK, Dad?" I asked, taking a seat beside him.

He took a deep breath. "I've been lethargic since the accident, and sore, but I'll recover. It takes longer when you get older. You'll see," he answered with his usual smile and a tiny spark in his eyes.

My mother watched us, her eyes bouncing from us to the TV. I turned towards it, moving my head turtle slow. The volume low, I read the bulletin running across the bottom of the screen. *Jess Thomas escaped from the ambulance after killing two paramedics and a state trooper after a near-death accident earlier today. She is considered dangerous.*

The news changed from the morbid scene to the newscaster. "There are more reports coming in of people attacking other people, biting into their flesh. Our phones are ringing off the hook. If you don't have to leave your house, don't! Stay inside," the newscaster urged in a desperate tone.

I stared, unblinking. Without turning my head I stated, "Do you believe me now? You've known her as long as I've known Sarah and she's not dangerous, but she's not her!"

My mom nodded, grabbing and clutching my father's hand. He nodded in agreement. "Let me pack us a few things," she stated and stood as someone pounded on our door. One minute they didn't believe me, the next Mom was packing a bag. The power of the news since it was announced to thousands of people, rather than a fifteen-year-old girl saying it, then it must be true.

Sarah's shaky, tear-filled voice outside confirmed it was her and Bryce. I flung the door open wide and she collapsed into my arms. "Maddie! She's one of them. Maddie, she's one of them," she sobbed. I walked her inside, followed by Bryce.

I sat Sarah on the couch and dabbed at her face with a tissue. "I'm sorry." At this point I forgot about my dad, solely focused on Sarah.

She continued to sob as Bryce paced back and forth. Noting his nerves I asked, "What is it?"

He tucked his arms behind his back and stopped pacing. "I went home and checked on my dad. He... he... didn't look right. His skin was pale and he kept muttering we-yak, we-yak, over and over. When he noticed me staring at him he charged me, yelling we-yak. His eyes were glassy and crazed. I just stood there until he grabbed my arm and bared his teeth. I... I... kicked him between the legs and he went down. Then I slammed the door on him and shoved a chair beneath the knob. I locked the house up tight before I left... him... there."

He sucked in a deep breath. "I left him there, Maddie! He's one of them!" he said, his voice trembling.

"I'm sorry Bryce," I said, offering him my hand. He didn't take it, but started pacing again.

My dad, still on the couch and not saying a word, finally spoke, "I'm sorry to hear about your father. I'm Bill, Maddie's father."

Bryce halted in front of him as if he hadn't noticed him until that moment and nodded, "I'm Bryce, a friend of Maddie's," then continued pacing.

"How do you know each other?" my dad asked, perching his chin on his folded hand.

My mom returned to the living room with a single duffle bag and her purse.

"This is Bryce, Mom. I'll explain everything when we get to safety. Right now, we need to leave."

She glanced at Sarah and joined our embrace. "I'm so sorry, Sarah. She was a good mom, a good person."

"I have my father's Pacifica, there's plenty of room for everyone," Bryce stated as we exited the house. It surprised me how easily my parents agreed to it. I guessed seeing someone they know zombified changed their minds. Let them know I wasn't insane, and assured me I wasn't dilly whackers in the head. I sank into the backseat with Sarah. Her arms wrapped tightly around me.

Out the window, I spotted my neighbor's tabby cat, sitting in the grass, his glowing eyes following the van as it drifted out of the driveway.

"Stop!" I hollered. He was in the dream. I didn't leave him then, and I wasn't going to now.

The van stopped. "What, Maddie?"

"The cat." I leaned Sarah onto my mom's shoulder and threw open the van door. He meowed at me when I scooped him up then I remembered we needed meds. I jogged back to the van and peeked inside. "I forgot something. Be back in a sec," I said, rolling the door closed.

The cat under one arm, I fumbled with my key in the lock. These things never worked when I was nervous or scared and I probably should have dropped the cat off in the van when I went back to it, but my brain wasn't processing like normal. I pushed the door open in a hurry and it hit the round, plastic wall protector. Jogging through the house, I dropped the cat onto my parents' bed, then grabbed the trash can in their bath, dumped its contents onto the floor and scooped all the various prescriptions and over-the-counter drugs into it.

A gunshot rang through my ears. I jumped, nearly dropping the trash can. I caught it between my knee and other hand then fumbled with it as I stuffed it under my arm and snatched the cat, stuffing him beneath the other, and sprinted towards the door -- my heart pounding like a hard rain. A gunshot meant a zombie. My premonition was becoming a very real -- too real -- reality.

Dark clouds were moving in fast, making the evening darker than usual. Even in the reigning blackness, I made out Bryce's form standing in the doorway. "Get in the van, Maddie, before more of them show up." He held a huge gun pointed in the air. Its barrel the length of my arm. Knowing little about guns, I assumed it was a shotgun. A trail of blood spilled across the sidewalk, leaking from a man. He lay face down in the grass and the back of his head had a huge, gaping, sloppy hole in it. Brain matter oozed out onto the lawn. I recoiled, giving his body a wide berth. *Yuck!*

Without stopping, I ran to the van. My mom slid the door open and I dropped the drug-filled trash can onto the floor along with the cat, then jumped inside. The cat meowed, then padded gingerly around our feet and onto Sarah's lap. She snuggled him to her chest as Bryce stepped into the van, handed my father the shotgun, and cranked the motor.

Chapter Four

Bryce drove past the closest freeway entrance; I assumed to avoid any traffic jams or zombie attacks. I glanced behind me. My mom had scooted into the third row, the duffle bag on the seat beside her. She gave me a weak smile as she sat, more silent than I'd ever seen her, but otherwise fine.

Bryce mentioned his family in the dream. The way he said it, I assumed he meant more than his father, but nobody else occupied the van, so where were they? He only mentioned his dad turning. Curious, I leaned forward. "Where's the rest of your family?"

"My mom took my younger sister with her to Italy. They're fine," he said, sounding annoyed.

"How do you know?" I glanced toward my father as he stared at me through pale, glassy eyes. I shifted my gaze back to Bryce and said in a low voice, "Weren't they in your dream?" I hadn't asked him about the details of his dream. I guess because most of it we shared, or I plum hadn't thought about it.

His voice curt, he responded, "Yes and they're fine, like I said. Once we get to the boat I'll call her."

I felt my dad's eyes on me and turned my head. "Maddie, he's driving. Leave him be."

I nodded and pushed backwards into my seat, when the van stopped abruptly. It jolted me forward, my shoulder hitting the back of my father's seat.

"And buckle up!" Dad ordered. After a deep breath of frustration he asked, "Where are we headed?"

The seatbelt clicked in place I responded to my father's question, "Your boat."

In a proud voice, he responded, "Ole Earnie. He'll take us anywhere over the water. A fine seaworthy sailboat he is." Most people identify their boat as a *she* but not my father. He always uses male pronouns as if the boat was actually a man.

Leave it to my dad to forget zombies and life or death situations and focus on his boat. I heard my mother release a slight sigh and I wondered if she thought the same thing I did. There was plenty of room in the van, but the tension between us made the drive take forever.

I gazed out the windshield as Bryce eased the van around two people standing in the street. They lurched forward, one rigid step after the next. Other than their strange movements, they appeared normal, not covered in blood or with their entrails dragging on the ground.

I glanced at Sarah who was staring at the cat while she petted his soft fur. He purred in response, so loud I heard it from the seat next to her. I was glad she wasn't watching out the window. She didn't need any reminders about her mom. I blinked back tears at the thought, while Bryce maneuvered the van through the zombies.

My eyes glued to them, one a woman, who stared blankly as we passed. She was fully intact. I turned towards the other, who, on closer inspection, was more obviously a victim before turning zombie. His button up shirt drooped off his shoulder and deep bites covered his neck.

We neared the marina when the dark sky opened up and rain beat against the van, water drizzling over the windows and Bryce turned the wipers on high to wipe it off the windshield. A gold truck and a white SUV were parked at the other end of the marina, but we didn't see any people.

"We should wait until the rain stops," suggested my mom, finally speaking.

My father agreed. Sarah and I sat quietly. I had plenty to say but chose to bite my tongue for the moment. The rain didn't bother me and I didn't think sitting in the van was the smartest idea. We were sitting ducks. I had the knife in my bag and wasn't afraid to stick a few rigor-stricken deaders in the head.

We all swapped glances, staring at each other when something beat against the window beside my father. We all jumped. My eyes widened as I stared at a man in a uniform. His bald head glowed from the marina lights. It glistened like a halo circling his round face. He shone a flashlight at us and motioned for my father to roll the window down.

He wasn't a zombie, as they lacked the brain power and intelligent thoughts. The rain outside slowed to a trickle as my father unrolled the window.

"Can we help you?"

"You need to get going. It's not safe out here," he said in a quivering voice as he chewed on a toothpick, swishing it from one side of his mouth to the other.

My father cleared his throat. "I have a vessel here," he said in his firm 'I mean business' voice.

"Have you checked it yet?"

"Not today. I know the owners and have docked my boat here for years. What's the problem?" my father asked, as if the apocalypse wasn't happening and life was hum-drum normal. I imagined his eyes narrowed as he studied the uniformed man. My guess was he was a rent-a-cop.

Bryce glanced at me from the corner of his eye. We'd checked it and knew it was locked tight. Even if zombies were on the boat, they weren't inside it.

The man's cheeks twitched as he let out an eerie laugh. "You won't be talking with the owners anymore," he said, pulling a gun and holding it to my father's face.

Bryce spoke then: "That baby blue one over there. That's ours."

"Get out, both of you," he turned the flashlight past my father and straight into my eyes. "Looks like you're planning a family vacation. The rest of you stay here." He moved the flashlight and an array of colored dots muddled my vision.

Bryce and my father swapped momentary glances. My father gulped as he unbuckled his seat belt and stepped out of the van. Bryce followed, and I watched in terror as they walked towards the baby blue yacht that was twice the size of my father's. The man followed behind, holding the gun to their backs.

I looked around. The shotgun was propped against the dash in front of my father's seat. I glanced toward my mom who shifted nervously. Her eyes fixed on me.

"Don't do it, Maddie," she ordered, as if she'd read my mind. Those days were over. Without looking back at her I climbed into the front seat.

Bryce and my father were in trouble. I had to do something, so I grabbed the gun, twisted in my seat, and brought it to my face. I'd never shot a gun other than in video games, but I'd seen tons of movies. It couldn't be that difficult. I clicked the lever thing on the topside of the gun. I knew that was the safety.

"Maddie, your father can handle him" she said, her voice quaking. I imagined her wringing her hands together like a dishrag.

From the corner of my eye, I watched Sarah lift her eyes off the cat and stare towards me. I met her gaze and she nodded her approval then mouthed, *Be careful.*

The men drew closer to the boat with each second I wasted. I pushed the door open, snuck around the side and observed my surroundings. I felt like a hunter in the wild carrying the big shotgun, but acted more like a detective on a cheesy cop show. As I moved around the van, I spotted a crate identical to the one where I found Bryce in my… our dream.

I scurried towards it, doing my best to step over and around the large puddles so as not to make splashing noises that would catch the creepy bald man's attention. Upon reaching it, I crouched. Placing my back against the wet wooden side, I slid

28

around it and onto my knees and peeked out. Bryce and my father stepped onto the boat, I used the man's shining head as a guiding light. He was still behind them.

Taking a deep breath, I moved back around the side and out of their view. The nose of the shotgun rose over the top as I held it straight and fired. Its recoil hit my upper thigh and I screamed as I doubled over, the gun hitting the ground. My leg throbbed and I knew I'd have a nasty bruise.

Weighty footsteps sloshed through the standing rainwater as I pulled myself together and glanced around the side of the crate. My face squeezed tight as I cringed from the ache flaring from my leg and spreading through my body. The man rushed towards me, the gun in his hand at his side. I stood, my leg unsteady, and held the gun towards him. I cocked it. Movie people always made the mistake of talking in real life. This was different, and he was a very genuine threat; there wasn't time to waste or think. I pulled the trigger and fired a shell. The sound cut through the silence and the man dropped to the ground.

I cocked it again and aimed straight towards him. He writhed in pain, holding his leg. Bryce and my father rushed towards him. Bryce sprinted like a gazelle; my father's movements were slow and unstable. Almost like he was a... I swallowed hard and squelched the thought. He was fine, going to be right as rain soon. I ran-limped around the crate, holding the gun downwards towards the bald, uniformed man struggling on the wet cement. It was a lucky shot that I hit him at all, but I didn't want him to know that or show my weakness.

Bryce snatched his gun while my dad knelt and spoke with the man. *Dad, no!* My hobble picked up as I moved towards them. My father glanced at me. "We need to get this man to the van and patch his leg."

Blood trickled from his blue rent-a-cop style pants. He twisted his head and glared at me. His eyes burned into mine. "You dumb girl! The noise attracts them."

How dare he even speak?! I pressed the barrel against his forehead. "You have no right to talk after holding my father and friend at gun point."

"It's empty," Bryce said, as he leaned over and grabbed it then flipped the chamber open.

"We don't have time for this. Don't you get it?" the man urged.

I jammed the gun against his skull. My dad glanced at me and shoved the gun off his head. "Get back to the van, get your mom and Sarah. We're leaving," he stated in a firm no-nonsense voice. "This man is coming with us."

I rolled my eyes and dragged myself towards the van, splashing hard through the standing rain puddles, cringing in pain with each step, but I tried not to let it show. *Drip drag drip drag* rang through my ears. I drew closer to the van. A shadow moved spastically through the darkness and a gentle waterfront breeze swept my hair back, sending a whiff of dead with it. *Oh crap!*

I lifted the gun and cocked it towards the menacing shadow. Maybe it wasn't a dead person, maybe it was still alive, only hurt. In my dream I was Zombie Girl, a ruthless killing machine, but in real life I was a simple suburban teenager whose only killing experience was squashing bugs. I gathered my courage. If I could shoot at the man, I could shoot at the thing moving towards me.

I dragged myself close enough to see its glazed, blank eyes. It was a woman with short bobbed hair and a gaping hole in her chest surrounded by a crimson red stain. I lifted the shotgun and pulled at the trigger, but it jammed. *Crap!* And my knife was inside my backpack in the van.

She drew closer with each *drip drag*. In the dream, we didn't have guns but primitive weapons, and the zombies' movements were slow. I turned the gun around and ran towards her, forgetting the pain in my leg, and swung the butt at her head. Down she went, dropping like a brick.

I glared into her eyes as she growled at me. Positive she'd lost her humanity, I smashed the butt of the gun repeatedly against her skull until it was a mess of brain matter and blood. From behind, someone grabbed the gun as I stood above her, breathing heavily.

"Let's go, Zombie Girl." I turned to see Bryce's face wearing a somber expression, his trusty shovel in his hands. "Are you ready?"

I raised a brow. "What?"

He pointed his shovel past me. "They're coming."

My eyes traced his shovel. Several jerking shadows moved towards us and all I had was a jammed gun. It worked well enough to take down the zombie woman -- it would have to do. Bryce and I nodded at each other and sprang into action, his shovel whacking hard into the head of a man. He dropped and Bryce swung again.

I veered the gun at another, a chunk of flesh missing from its neck as if something had snacked on him. He collapsed, his hands reached for me, grazing my legs. I jumped back and smashed the gun with so much force his face it caved.

Another came at me, his arm dangling by a thread ligament. *Yuck!* I took him down, and then another. They stank like maggoty trash. I cringed as I struck another, pounding the gun butt into its skull until it stopped wriggling.

"Overkill. He's gone. Impressive work with the butt of a rifle," said Bryce in a low voice.

Rifle? What was the difference between a rifle and a shotgun? They were both large guns and I assumed a shotgun would do just as much damage as the rifle I held in my hand.

I glanced at the bloody mess that was left of his skull, then the impressive pile of zombies and counted. *Eight, we'd taken down eight.* It was a surreal moment as Bryce grabbed my hand and we sprinted back to the van. I slid the door open. "Now's our chance, let's go."

My parents and Sarah stared at me with widened eyes.

"That was amazing, Maddie," voiced Sarah in an I-can't-believe-it voice.

My lips involuntarily turned upward into a smile as I reached for my mother's hand to assist her out of the third-row seat.

Once out of the van, she wrapped her arms around me. "How did you…? I didn't know you…" She stumbled over her words.

With the rain gone, the air was muggier, and steam rose from the river, giving the entire marina an unnerving atmosphere. "It's OK, Mom," I said, "we don't have time. We need to go."

She nodded.

Bryce in the lead with the shovel and my father at the tail with the rifle he took from me and unjammed while we scurried towards the boat. The man I shot gimping along with us. I guess we couldn't leave him and it appeared he wasn't hurt so badly he wouldn't survive. The blood no longer leaked from his wound. My thigh ached with each step as I ran-limped and something pointy in my pocket poked at the sorest spot on my leg making the pain shoot through my entire body.

Bryce climbed on board first, assisting my mom who, in turn, helped the rest of us as Bryce hurriedly pulled up the anchor and untied the boat. He climbed the stairs, followed by my father, and the engine cranked, sputtered, then caught.

The pain in my leg was a dull ache as I stuffed my hand into my pocket and pulled out a set of keys. My father's set to *Earnest Earl.* Sarah and my mom held each other. Their wild eyes searched my face as I shuffled past them, unlocked the cabin door and saw them downstairs.

The unmistakable rumble of another boat pounded in my ears as I quick-checked each room. I limped onto the deck. The man stood on it, staring straight through the fog ahead at another boat, a few feet larger, heading towards us. It was moving so quick the water spray caused waves to hit our boat as we cut a sharp left.

I lost my balance and fell against one of the benches. Luckily, my good leg hit the deck first, padding the fall for my sore leg. The man braced himself, wrapping his hands around the railing, as his legs slid and he screamed in pain.

From the other boat, blank, glassy, lifeless eyes stared at us as spray from our boat washed over his face and he fell over the railing, his back a mess of blood and tangled flesh. He hit the water like a sack of rocks and sank.

"I wasn't planning on harming anyone," said the man after several seconds, breaking our silence.

I glanced at him. His forehead wrinkled, he met my gaze. "You held my father at gunpoint!"

He stumbled over his words. "It... it was empty. I just wanted to get away and," his eyes shot toward the deck, "I didn't want to kill any more of those things."

Anger seethed inside me as I realized what he meant. "No! You wanted my family to do it. Why risk your own life, right? Oh no! Risk a stranger's life instead!"

He pulled himself into a sitting position, resting his back against the railing. "I didn't think of it like that. But you are a veritable killing machine. If I'd have known that, I'd have taken you instead."

Clenching my jaw, I stared him down. I remembered him ordering the rest of us to stay in the van. He was simply hoping to survive in what had become a dangerous world in a few short hours. It was survive or die, and I couldn't be angry because he wanted to live. "Why don't we take a look at that leg?"

Chapter Five

Bryce at the helm, the man and I hobbled downstairs. I grabbed the first aid kit and tore open an antiseptic packet. I dabbed at the blood on his leg as he spoke, "I'm Jack. Jack Glenny." He tilted his head and his cheek pinned up in a cringe. "I worked at the marina for twelve years. I've never seen anything like this. I don't have an explanation for what's happening. I show up for the night shift, same as I do five days a week, and in the office I see the owner's wife, Jenna, eating her husband, Harvey. What's the world coming to?"

He asked as if I had any answers. I was simply a teen girl trying to save her family. His eyes watered as I met his gaze. "I don't know."

His gaze shifted down as I wrapped a bandage over his leg. "But you… you seem like maybe you know something."

I sighed. "The bullet only grazed you, so you should be good in a day or two."

I stood to put the kit away, he grabbed my hand. "What about you?"

I wasn't sure if he meant 'what do you know' or was asking about my own wound. My bruise was in a place he certainly would never see and no doubt would heal itself in a day or two and I didn't like or trust him enough to tell him about the premonition. "It'll heal," I said, wrenching my hand away.

My dad staggered from his bedroom. At first I thought he'd turned until he sat at the table across from Jack and said. "Maddie, your mom and Sarah are resting. Now's the time to put our heads together and come up with a plan." Like clockwork the door to the cabin opened and in walked Bryce.

"I talked with my mom. She and my sister are heading back to her family's home. They were in the airport! Do you believe that, in the airport while all this is going on?" He took a breath and wiped his palms down his jeans. "Their flight was delayed and I told her strange things were happening. So I put Earnest Earl on a course to Italy."

Jack stood. "You what? This boat can't handle those waters. You're going to kill us!"

"Wow!" my dad countered. The strength he used to form the word and unleash it with intensity seemed to drain the life out of him. His pale eyes drooped as he worked to form each of his next words. "He's a seaworthy boat and if we're careful and don't hit any storms we'll be in plenty good shape to get to Italy."

I stood quiet, watching the menfolk do their thing and beat their chests, and observed my father - - far too many chiefs and testosterone in the cabin. The only woman in the room, I had to be the estrogenized voice of reason. I cleared my throat in the same way my mother would. "A plan?" I asked, raising my brows and smiling.

Three sets of male eyes peered at me as if they'd all forgotten I was in the room. "Yes," agreed my father.

Within a few minutes they'd devised a working plan. Bryce would take first shift steering the boat, which, oddly, nobody was currently at the helm, and Jack would take second shift. I jumped on third shift, beating my father to it. *He needs rest, lots of rest.* I walked with him, arm in arm, to the bedroom. With a struggle, his body stiff, he lay down next to my mom.

I remembered throwing his muscle relaxers into the trash can at home on my medicine raid. Going to it now I found them and opened a bottle of water. I strolled past Jack who was already asleep on the bench that folded into a sleeper. The boat wasn't big but it slept six comfortably.

I stuffed the pills in my dad's mouth and brought the water bottle to his lips. He drank then eased backwards onto the pillow. "I love you, Dad," I whispered.

"I'll be fine, Maddie, and I love you," he whispered in response as I pulled out the trundle and lay down just beneath him.

"Maddie, Maddie," called my mother from the other side of a long dark tube.

"Mom, where are you?" I called. "I can't see you."

"Open your eyes, Maddie."

I slid my eyes open to my mother's worried face. Deep wrinkles like I'd never seen embedded in her forehead. "Mom," I sat up, placing my palm against her wet cheek. "What is it?"

She sniffled but kept her voice low, "Honey, I think, I think your father. Umm," she drew her tongue across her lips as her eyes shifted to the bed.

I leapt from the trundle. "Dad, Dad," I said urgently, shaking him.

"Maddie, stop. He's gone, Maddie. His body is cold." Her eyes went from sorrow-filled to wild in a split second. "We need to be quiet. That man is asleep on the other side of the curtain and I don't trust him," she whispered in a harsh tone.

I put two fingers against my father's wrist and felt for a pulse – nothing. I pressed my hand against his forehead and it was cold, not freezing, but it didn't radiate the heat it should. Desperate, I brought the two fingers to his neck and felt. I waited, holding in my tears and my breath. My dad couldn't be dead or one of the deaders stalking around. He was my dad -- strong, courageous, and indestructible.

There it was, a thump. I waited and another thump. "He's still alive, Mom," I said, squeezing my eyes to stop the flow of tears and wrapping my arms around her. "He's alive, but barely. His pulse is weak."

"Are you sure?" she asked through her tears.

"Mom, do you think he's turning into a…" I couldn't say it, even though I knew it. There was no other explanation. Sure, his heart was beating, but the thumps were far apart, not fast like a living, healthy person.

Her wild eyes shifted around the room. "No, no, hold on," she walked to the pull-out wall drawers and grabbed something from the top one. In the dark I couldn't tell what it was until she drew closer to me.

"Pantyhose?"

"We can use these to tie him to the bed," she stated, holding her head high.

We were going to tie my father to the bed that had no bed posts. How on earth were we going to do that? He still had a pulse, but for how long? *Is this how they died and came back?*

She was already ripping her pantyhose as I stood and placed my hand over hers to stop her. "Mom, there are no bed posts."

"Then we'll be creative."

My mom had gone bananas and so had I as we worked as a team to tie my father's wrists together along with his ankles. It was ludicrous insanity but, like my mother, I didn't want to believe that this was the end of the road for the man who made me Saturday pancakes and bacon, taught me to ride a bike, and was finally accepting that I was an almost grown up person.

We finished and took a step back, eyeing our handy work. He wasn't going anywhere. My mom was especially proud of how she'd rigged the pantyhose around his wrists to the pull-out dresser drawers. My dad hadn't moved voluntarily once but I'd felt a warm breath or two while working on his wrists. Whether it was the drugs I gave him or his body changing, he was knocked out, and due to be ripe and madder than a wasp when he woke up... if he woke up.

"We can't tell anyone, Maddie. This is our secret."

She'd lost it, gone completely over the edge. "We need to tell Bryce," I insisted.

"You can tell Bryce, but that man, he can't know. He'll kill him for sure," she urged, her face solemn, replacing her crazed expression.

We turned our heads simultaneously to a rustling on the other side of the curtain. That meant Jack was up. I put my finger to my lips then whispered directly into my mom's ear, "His name is Jack. I don't trust him either, but if he's up that means Bryce will be off duty soon."

Her eyebrows lowered. "Off duty," she mouthed.

I nodded in response. We waited side by side, lying on the little trundle, until we heard Jack leave the cabin. A few minutes passed that felt like hours and the cabin door opened again. I peeked out the curtain to see Bryce.

"Psst," I said, holding my finger to my mouth for him to stay quiet, my other hand holding the curtain.

He followed the noise and stared at me with blank, questioning eyes. I motioned for him to join me. Slowly he walked my way. I opened the curtain wider and he joined us in the little room. His eyes stared ahead at my father, then to my mom, then to me.

Chapter Six

"What's going on here?" Bryce asked.

We told him the story and, even as I said it, I knew I should have simply put a spiked tool to my father's brainstem, but I couldn't. He was my father and he still had a heartbeat and he was still breathing, so technically he was still alive, only drugged heavily and tied up.

I thought more about the entire zombie illness that swept through the city. The brainstem controlled all the involuntary actions such as digestion, heartbeat, breathing, the stuff that happens in our bodies that we never consciously think about and cutting them off at the brainstem was an effective death. *So did zombies have thought processes?* They growled instead of talked. They heard noises. Jack warned us against the noises when I fired the rifle. *Can they see or do they know only because of sound?* I flip-flopped the thought over and over in my head.

After a couple minutes, oblivious to anything but what was on my mind, I remembered Bryce mentioned his father talking after he turned, saying 'we-yak'. *Did that mean something? And how did he talk if he turned and, heck, how did they turn?*

I scrambled into the kitchen and sifted through the top drawer. I knew my mom kept a pad of paper there. When I found it, and a pen, I ran to the bathroom and grabbed the thermometer then back into the bedroom. Bryce and my mom stared at me with narrowed eyes.

"What are you doing?" asked Bryce.

"I think I have something, maybe. Listen carefully, a zombie's brainstem works, maybe even their cerebellum and temporal lobe, but those are the most ancient parts of our brains. We know they hear, but can they see? They can't reason or talk. So Dad's heart will keep beating and he'll keep breathing. Mom, take this notepad and record his pulse every two hours." All that rolled off my tongue so fast that I didn't take a breath until it was all out and I shoved the notepad, pen, and thermometer into my mom's hands.

My mom looked at me curiously but said nothing as she took the items. Her eyes then shifted towards my father, tied and bound by pantyhose on the bed.

"Slow down. Maddie. Are you suggesting we study your father?" he asked with raised brows.

That was a great question, but my answer dismayed even me. I needed a reason to keep him alive. *Great! All I needed now was a white lab coat and pocket protector and I'd be a certified loony scientist.* "Yes, in a manner of speaking."

The room was silent for several long seconds that felt like several long hours. Their eyes stared at me, unwavering, until I finally spoke again, avoiding the entire test-dad-subject. I looked Bryce square in the eye. "You said your dad turned but talked. He said something like 'we-yak'. It has to mean something for his brain to hold onto that phrase.

Think Bryce. I can't be the only one with answers, we have to work together."

My mom's eyes left me and trailed to my father. She then opened the notepad and pressed her fingers to my father's neck.

Bryce stumbled over his words as he shifted uneasily on his feet. "I don't know what it means."

"Think, Bryce. You said your dad is an environmental scientist. A project he's working on -- maybe?"

"OK, Maddie. I'll play with it. Maybe it means something," he said, hanging his head in sadness, then left the room.

I gazed at my father and understood the sorrow that comes with losing a parent. Mine lay on the bed but was no more my father than his was the last time he saw him.

Chapter Seven

We managed to keep my father and his condition under wraps. We brought Sarah in to help my mom. They took shifts taking his vital signs and kept up with medicating him. They even worked out a system to feed him water intravenously and used female menstruation pads beneath him to soak up any bodily function leakage. We all took turns moving and massaging his legs and arms. My mom insisted it would keep his blood flowing. I didn't know how long this would last or when we should let the drugs wear off but he was hydrated and alive.

I gazed over the vast ocean. We were a speck of nothing, floating on the water. A shadow brushed over me and I wrapped my hands around my chest and shivered, then it went away and the bright sun was beating against my head again.

I gazed upward and the sky, almost divided in the middle, was sunny and bright on one side with a couple puffy clouds but the other side was dark and foreboding. Heavy clouds thick with moisture hung low.

Over the past several days, Bryce had spoken with his mom each day and encouraged her to stay inside. She'd kept her eyes on the news and didn't have much to report from Italy. Life was still going on as normal until last night. She gave him her first report of violence. A man had wandered onto a school's grounds and taken a bite out of the shoulder of a teacher who'd noted the man wandering around the campus and urged him to leave. The violence in the states was all over the international news now. *It was spreading, but how?*

The sound of Bryce's and Jack's voices from overhead brought me out of my deep thought. They were discussing rerouting the boat to avoid the storm. I glanced at the sky again then wandered inside. The menfolk could figure it out. I had more important things on my mind. Sarah and the cat sat on the built-in sofa. She punched buttons on the radio and static squawked at her.

"I can't get a station. Did Bryce talk with his mom yet today?" Sarah asked with concern.

I shrugged. "I don't think so. I didn't ask," I answered, sitting on the sofa beside her and folding my legs beneath me. I clicked the TV that had been getting intermittent reception, static blazed from each channel and snow covered the screen. The barely audible squawks and deformed figures of yesterday were absent.

"I'm worried, Maddie. Every day, more and more stations become static. I'm beginning to think we're the only people left alive in the entire world, except Bryce's family. I feel so isolated." She rubbed her palm against the velour of the sofa. I glanced around for the cat. When he wasn't in Sarah's lap or purring in her ear he sat in the window of the bedroom Sarah slept in. I figured that's why my mom's allergies hadn't acted up unless there never were any allergies and they used it as an excuse not to have any pets.

"It sure feels that way, but there are others out there."

Her voice broke my pet thoughts. My mom strolled out of the bedroom, humming, and went straight to the kitchen where she pulled lunch meat, sliced cheese, butter, pickles, and various other condiments out of the fridge. She grabbed a pan and cut off a huge chunk of butter and dropped it in where it slowly melted.

Mom stopped humming then said, "Sarah, honey, can you grab the bag of French fries out of the freezer and spread them on a pan? Maddie, why don't you set the table." She continued humming as she prepared our lunch.

We didn't have gourmet meals, but mom made it work. She inventoried the kitchen and doled it out to make it last as long as possible, but when she'd opened the fridge I noticed how empty it was getting. Mom didn't complain; she did what she needed to. All the normal luxuries in life were gone now. It was survival but we'd need food, and soon, before we made it to Italy.

I set the table then went onto the deck and up the stairs where Bryce and Jack were still debating and planning a course of action.

As I grew closer Jack mentioned, "The heavy wind has us cruising at 31 knots."

"We're making good time but it's not fast enough," Bryce said nervously.

I cleared the ladder and stepped onto the top deck. Bryce's green eyes smiled when they met mine. "Hi, Maddie," he said as I halted beside him.

"What's up?" I asked, my eyes darting from Bryce to Jack. I knew Bryce was anxious about his mom and sister but was trying to lighten the mood.

"We've lost radar," Jack stated after clearing his throat.

"Really? The radio is static too and we've completely lost TV; nothing. It's like the world is dead."

Bryce swallowed hard. "I can't get hold of my mom either."

My eyes widened into cereal bowls. We were alone, alone in the world. "We need to make a stop soon too and load up on supplies. Mom's been rationing everything and isn't complaining but we're getting low."

Jack snorted and asked, "How's your dad?"

The first time he asked we told him he was sore from the accident and suffering sea sickness. He cocked his head and arched his brows but seemed to accept it. Now he gave me a similar look as I responded, "He's better but still weak."

"Hmm. We could use him, hope he's over it soon." Then he put his leg over the side and went down the stairs, leaving me and Bryce alone. Since we boarded the boat, with six of us and a cat, we hadn't been alone at all.

I sat beside him in the extra seat and propped my legs up. Darkness hung in the sky to the north. "So what's the plan?"

"Head south and hope to get close to Africa. The winds are giving us top speeds. Without weather or radar we can only assume the storm is coming from the US and heading east so if we continue south maybe we'll miss it," he stated, turning his head and gazing into my eyes.

I shifted my gaze upwards and tilted my head back. "The storm looks like it's coming from the north which means it's heading south toward us."

He held his pointer finger in the air above his head. "The wind is blowing east."

I lifted the chain of the compass and peered at it then glanced at the strange sky again and tilted the compass so Bryce could see. "Then the storm is heading for us. There's no way to escape it," I said with a sigh, having no knowledge yet how small this boat really was in the huge Atlantic and how devastating a storm could be.

He glanced at the compass then touched my hand. Changing the subject he asked, "How's your dad really doing?"

"About as good as the storm. His pulse has been steady at ten to fifteen beats a minute. His body is cold to the touch but staying at a steady sixty-eight degrees Fahrenheit. He has no color and is still drugged and tied. I don't even know if it's the drugs keeping him from turning completely or if his body is somehow finding a way to fight this," I said with a long sigh.

He wrapped his fingers around my hand and I wrapped mine around his as we stared into the dark sky above us. A tiny boat with six occupants, lost somewhere in the ocean, and a massive storm heading our way.

"Did you get a chance to talk to your mom today?"

"Nope, no service."

"How did we lose everything in a day and where did this zombie sickness come from? Why aren't we affected?"

He brushed a chunk of hair from his eyes. "I ask myself the same questions."

I shivered from the chilly wind the storm was bringing. He uncurled his fingers from mine and draped them around my shoulder, pulling me closer to him. I melted in that moment and hoped my mom didn't come up the stairs.

"Did I catch you at the wrong moment?" came a male voice and a maniacal chuckle. Maybe it wasn't maniacal but just sounded that way to me as Jack stepped onto the top deck and joined us. The first large rain drop hit my head. Its cold tendrils rolled through my hair, taking a crooked path.

Chapter Eight

Over the next few hours the boat was tossed over the water's surface and a huge wave nearly swallowed the lot of us. The boat sailed beneath its gigantic jaws as they closed above us. Jack steered the ship and we sailed across its tongue as if we were a surfer and came through the opening as its massive jaws clenched shut and sent us spiraling over the next waves. We managed to get the sails and masts down in enough time, but I worried as the waves pitched us across the ocean.

A bout of nausea tried to sneak up on me, vomit resting in my throat, but I couldn't be sick. So far the trip had been pleasant and, even though I lied to Jack, no one had suffered seasickness. Jack turned out to be great at steering us through the storm. At one point I held onto the rail, attempting to keep my dinner down, rain pelting on my head, and asked him where he learned to steer. He responded 'the coast guard'; he'd spent twenty years with them. I think he said twenty, but it might have been something else, the pounding of torrential rain and smashing of waves rocking the creaking boat made communication difficult.

After I stole back downstairs -- really I stumbled down the stairs -- the ferocious ocean tossing me into the cabin door which I grasped and turned, then literally fell down the steps. My mom standing at the bottom, her legs spread wide for balance and her hands on her hips. She glared at me. "I told you not to leave the cabin."

I gave her a quirky smile. "I uh…"

She took her hands off her hips and placed a palm on the wall beside her for balance then handed me a small pinkish pill. "It's a Dramamine. Take it; you'll feel better."

Still on the floor by my mother's feet I took the little pill, gathered up my saliva and forced it down with a ball of spit. "Thanks."

She offered me her hand and lifted. At that moment the boat hit a wave hard. The bow of Earnest Earl groaned as if it was about to split in two. My mom lost her balance and fell on top of me. Immediately she rolled off me and we shared a smile then crawled toward the sofa where Sarah sat with the cat. He was balled up in her lap with his head tucked beneath his body. I guess boats aren't natural spaces for cats.

I climbed onto the sofa and swept the curtain back, searching for any sign of Bryce, but didn't see him. Rain beat so hard against the window it was impossible to see anything but the rivulets and splashes hitting the glass. I hoped he was OK. The three of us and the cat stayed huddled together on the sofa until the water calmed and the boat stopped rocking and swaying.

The cabin door opened then and Bryce walked in. My heart pattered in happiness. He was alright, even though he was soaked from head to toe. His hair clung to his face and tendrils of water rushed over his wet body. I jumped off the sofa, feeling a bit guilty I was safe and dry, and grabbed him a towel. I wanted to pat his body down and strip the wet clothes off him but kept that little fantasy to myself as I tossed the towel nonchalantly at him.

He patted his face. "Thanks, Zombie Girl. The worst of the storm is over. We're in shallow water somewhere close to land, we think. We dropped the anchor and will check it out in the morning."

Jack walked into the cabin then and I saluted him. He saluted back. Maybe he wasn't so bad.

"You two must be starved. Let me fix you a bite before you sleep," offered my mom, jumping off the couch and rifling through the fridge.

Jack nodded and grabbed a handful of dry clothes. He was about the same size as Dad so Mom had brought him a few of Dad's things to wear. It wasn't like Dad needed them right now. He slipped into the bathroom and Bryce into Sarah's room. That's where he kept his stuff, but slept on the sofa in the living room.

All of us living this tight we learned to sleep through snoring and ignored the weird idiosyncrasies we each had such as Jack sounded like a jack-hammer when he slept and always rubbed his bald head as if he still had hair. Bryce always scraped silverware along his teeth when he ate and Sarah spent far too long in the bathroom.

I snuck off to the bedroom and left everyone in the living and kitchen area. Dad lay on the bed. The pantyhose tie Mom used to keep him on the bed had ripped during the storm, but somehow Dad was still on the bed. I shrugged and checked the notepad.

53

Mom last pumped muscle relaxers into him six hours ago so I took two more, noting two left in the bottle and crushed then stuffed them into my father's mouth then poured water into it. Some trickled down his throat and a little trailed over the corners of his lips and down his chin. I watched the white pills dissolve with the water as he involuntarily swallowed them. After I closed his mouth I sank into the comfort of the trundle and drifted to sleep.

Chapter Nine

Bright morning light streamed through the window. Not a sign that last night, between the ocean and storm, we almost died.

I strolled onto the deck to survey the damage and heard voices. As I strode toward the voices something squished beneath my foot causing me to lose my balance and I slid forward into the railing. I glanced back and spotted the culprit -- a fish; its guts pushing out from beneath its scales. On close inspection it was dead -- dead as in dead, not zombified. His gills didn't move at all. So fish could die. Maybe whatever the illness was it only affected humans. I grabbed a shovel and tossed his flattened, grotesque body back into the ocean.

Finding the source of voices, it was Jack and Bryce, the sun reflecting off Jack's bald head. The deck didn't have any apparent damage, I noted as I looked around. I supposed they already cleaned it up. Their backs were to me as they stared ahead, their elbows resting on the side of the boat. I strolled behind them and pushed my way between them.

"So what's up? Earnest Earl sustain any damage?" I asked a moment too early; before us was land. Not island land but land as far as the eye could see -- beach and what looked like tiny little buildings.

"Where are we?" I corrected.

Bryce shrugged. "The boat is fine. It's a seaworthy beast but we lost navigation completely.

Your guess is good as mine, but I think Africa. Morocco maybe."

My mouth gaped open.

"Let's eat and go," stated Jack firmly while glancing at Bryce. They'd become pretty cozy lately and that worried me. I also didn't like being ignored and was darn good at slaying zombies.

"I'm coming with," I stated matter-of-factly as I followed them inside. Besides food, we needed medicine for my dad too, but I didn't mention that.

Jack shrugged. "You have skill, we can use you," he said as he walked to the kitchen, pulled a mug from the cabinet, and poured coffee.

Within the hour we checked the lifeboat for damage and verified it was seaworthy. Boarding the tiny vessel we were soon on it, paddling to the shore line, and pulling the boat onto the sandy shore. We left my mom and Sarah onboard the boat. So far, we hadn't seen a soul in the water and were pretty sure there was no one else out there.

I grabbed my ax in one hand, Bryce hauled his head-chopping shovel, and Jack carried the rifle which I thought was stupid. Once it ran out of ammo, which had to be loaded, it would only serve as a blunt, thunking weapon when using the butt to give the blow.

I grabbed my knife just in case. We padded through the sand, our ears on alert, but heard nothing except the gentle rhythm of the surf. We made it further onshore to a street filled with shops; none were open. That wasn't a good sign. However, still no zombies.

Jack, who was in the lead, put his hand up for us to stop then he pointed to his ear and towards a shop to our left. He side-walked, holding his rifle out towards the building. On the other side a face pushed against it, bloodied, and dragged itself along the window, leaving a crimson streak. Jack, who wasn't as brave as he thought, jumped back and screamed like a girl. Soon enough the shuffling started. *Drip drag, drip drag.*

I was grateful they weren't any faster here in Africa. No, I scanned the store signs and recognized Playa. *We were in Spain? How the...* my thought was cut off as the first zombie reached us. Its jaw missing a chunk so its tongue hung from the side of its mouth. It jerked and stumbled towards us, the one at the window still scraping and clawing to get out and eat us up. After the zombie dropped from Bryce's leg to its chest he thrust the shovel into its neck and twisted.

I jumped in as three more headed our way. Their bodies spasming as they jerked forward. "Shoot them," I called to Jack as I thrust the hatchet into an old woman's brainstem. She had bites all over her face which made me realize that all the zombies we'd seen thus far had more than one bite. I didn't know how or if that meant anything.

I spun and took down another, then glanced at Jack through my peripheral vision. He stood frozen to the ground as if a statue. "Jack!" I called, running towards him as a dark-haired man with a blood covered Speedo and several chest bites cocked his head to sink his teeth in. *Yuck! His wrinkled, ashy skin hung in globs around the white band of the Speedo.* I didn't trust Jack for an unknown reason, maybe it was how we met. It didn't matter; he was still alive and not becoming a zombie today!

I kicked the dark-haired man in the ribs and he stumbled backwards and dropped, then I snatched Jack's gun from his hands and smashed the zombie's head until his brains coated the ground. I grabbed Jack by the arm and shook. "You were almost zombie food!"

"What?" he asked, half dazed.

I wondered how he survived the coast guard as I shoved the rifle back into his hands. "Use this to shoot them in the head."

He nodded in response as I swung my ax and caught the topless woman behind me in the neck, dropping her to the ground. Her head attached by jagged threads as blood pooled beside her.

I turned my ax at the ready, searching for more, but we cleared them, the ones in the streets anyways. The ones in the buildings pawed at the glass, trying to get to us.

"Were not in Africa, but that's good because I can read some Spanish. That store over there is the US equivalent to a Jiffy store on the beach," I said, ax in hand as I led the group.

We stopped in front of the store and Bryce spoke, "Jack, you alright? We can't have you freezing up. We need you."

Jack nodded and nervously switched the rifle to his other hand. "I won't. I don't know what happened but I'm here now."

"I'll go in first; Zombie Girl, you come in after me. Jack, while we're clearing the front, you check the back," he paused for a second. "All you have to do is shoot their heads or jam the butt into their faces. They go down easy."

At that moment I felt bad for Jack. It was the second time I'd had sympathy for the man. I noted that as Bryce went inside to the left and I followed on his heels to the right. We swung and chopped while Jack went between us directly to the back.

A loud boom rang through my ears as he fired the rifle. The front zombies cleared, I ran to the back with Bryce beside me. A large man with raw meat in his hands and face lay in a heap on the floor, next to him was the site of the raw meat.

"H-e-l-p," said a tiny voice from the source of the large zombie man's snack. A girl, no older than me, dragged herself towards us with her only arm. The other had clearly been pulled from its socket. Only strips of bloody flesh and muscle hung from her shoulder. My heart was drawn to her, but with the multiple bites, missing body parts and a chunk of face flesh that included her right ear torn from her she would be a zombie in a matter of time.

I knew what we had to do even though none of us wanted to do it. Our eyes shifted from one to the next and then back to her as she reached her one good arm upward, her head falling against the cement stock room floor.

I pulled the knife out of my pocket. It was the best weapon for this compassion killing. I walked towards her, knife in my shaky hand. Bryce grabbed my wrist with one hand. "I'll do it," he offered.

Sniffling a little, I handed him the knife. He quickly jabbed it upward into the girl's neck beneath the hairline. My suppressed tears snuck to the corners of my eyes and fell over my cheeks. Bryce wiped the knife and handed it back to me. A single, sexy man tear dropped from his eye. I adored sensitive men. *How sensual!*

Without words, we dragged the bodies outside because they reeked like the rotten flesh that they were. The big guy took all three of us. I turned to go back into the store and from the corner of my eye I spotted something moving. I whipped myself around to see a bottle had rolled out of the big man's pocket. A little medicine bottle; my Spanish wasn't good enough to read what it was for so I picked it up and stuffed it into my pocket and it gave me another idea.

I went through all their pockets and personal items looking for anything of value. That sounded pretty stupid since I didn't think anything had any real value in the zombie world except life. However, a couple gold rings, a few colorful euros, and two bottles of medication might add up to something, somewhere along the way.

Bryce and Jack were already collecting boxes and stuffing them with canned and boxed goods, shampoo, soap, water bottles, toilet paper, and anything else we thought we could use. I went up and down every aisle searching for any kind of medication but came up empty - not a single bottle of aspirin, ibuprofen - not even cough syrup. It puzzled me. *Did grocery stores in other countries not have pharmaceuticals?* I let the thought go. I'd keep my eyes peeled for a pharmacy.

Jack made himself useful and found a flatbed. He rolled it towards us. Its wheels creaking as they moved. "That doesn't look too sturdy," said Bryce as he walked towards it and took the handle, rolling it to and fro.

"I can fix it up. Beats walking it all by hand," countered Jack. "Help me turn it upside down. I saw some tools under the front counter."

I sat on a box and popped open a water bottle, nearly guzzling the whole thing at once.

"Thirsty," chuckled Bryce, "can you hand me one… please?" He sat on another box and stretched his long legs.

"Break time?" questioned Jack as he returned with a small box in his hands.

"Yup," I said, grabbing a bag of chips and pulling it open, "we killed the zombies, you get the cart."

"Deal," Jack said with a smile. It was the first time I'd seen him smile and at that moment I started to like him.

About thirty minutes later, Bryce jumped in and helped Jack with the cart. I took the liberty of stretching my legs and walked around the small store. I felt like a mall walker, one of the old people that stroll the mall every morning. Every mall in the US had some. I reached the frozen section and longed for the cool, smooth yet sweet taste of ice cream but what was there wasn't ice cream and it wasn't frozen anymore. The contents of flan and other delicious Spanish deserts spilled from their packages and pooled in the bottom.

My mouth watered as my mind envisioned a chocolate shake with milk chocolate drizzled on top and whipped cream piled so high it dribbled around the glass holding it. A loud, shrill screech brought my mind back from milkshake heaven and made me jump.

My first instinct, I ran to the storeroom in the back, thinking that a zombie was hidden somewhere and popped out taking a bite of someone's flesh. Bryce and Jack were still working on the cart and intact. No surprise zombie attack.

"Did you guys hear that?" I asked with no response. I stepped closer and cleared my throat. "Did you hear that?"

"What?" asked Bryce as he turned a screw for a fresh shiny new wheel into the wooden bottom of the cart. A dribble of sweat trailed between his eyes and down his nose then over his lips. My mind flashed to his kissable lips on mine. I shook it from my head.

"I heard a scream. Neither of you heard it?" As the words left my lips, more screams followed. Our glances shifted from one to the next, then I charged into the store, stopping behind a tall structure used to hold fruit which, by the smell, was going rotten.

A hand touched my shoulder. "Right behind you," responded Bryce.

I turned my head, our widened eyes met but not in a passionate moment, instead a moment of premonition recognition and *red-eyed monkeys*.

"What?" asked Jack.

Our eyes shifted, our locked gaze moved towards him. "Mon-keys," answered Bryce, pronouncing it one syllable at a time.

"Well, heck, monkeys don't kill people. By the looks on your faces you'd think an army of something worse than zombies was out there. I don't get it." Jack said, scratching his bald head.

"When's the last time you saw a red-eyed monkey?" I questioned, my eyes staring straight into his.

The intensity of my gaze seemed to make him nervous as he shuffled his feet. "I guess I've never seen a monkey other than at the zoo and, well, they didn't have red eyes."

Another shrill scream broke through the air around us, so high-pitched it rang for several seconds in my ears. As an automatic response against the pain, I clutched my hands over my ears.

Chapter Ten

Meanwhile on Earnest Earl...

Maddie's mom, Angie, checked her husband's pulse; no change. She recorded it and looked longingly at the man she loved. She'd given him the last bit of muscle relaxers they had that morning. Now she waited for him to wake up and wondered whether he'd be her husband or... something else. She noted his cheeks had more color and touched her hand to them; still cool.

"Angie!" called Sarah with urgency as her steps pounded against the boat deck and down the steps.

Angie lifted herself off the bed and met Sarah at the opening to the bedroom as she drew the curtain back. "What is it, honey?" Sarah had almost been a second daughter to her and the tone and rush in the girl's voice worried her, but the look on her face said something else -- her brown eyes wide and her face smiling.

"A ship, a big ship, like a military carrier or something. Come!" She grabbed Angie's hand and dragged her onto the top deck, stuffing the binoculars in her chest. "Over there." She pointed.

Sure enough, Angie put the binoculars on and found the ship easily. It was huge but the writing was too small; she couldn't make out what was written on it or what country, only that it did indeed look like a military ship. She dropped the binoculars.

64

"I don't think they see us. Should we shoot off a flare...?" Sarah suggested, her voice trailing off as she realized they couldn't do that. If it was a military carrier with soldiers they'd discover Mr. Whyte and that wouldn't be good. She quickly followed up with, "I know we can't do that. I'm sorry. I was so excited to know that we aren't alone. There are other people alive. Maybe the ship is filled with uninfected people they're talking to a safe place."

Angie gazed into Sarah's hopeful brown eyes. She watched the sparkle leave as she understood they couldn't let the ship know they were there, but it wasn't only because of her husband. They didn't know what was on that ship. They could be carrying infected. It could be a run-away ship. She took another look, then got an idea.

"It's better for us they don't know we're here, but we can keep track of them, watch where they're heading, and I can figure out where we are in the meantime." The ship was following a path vertical to where they sat, not north or south. West, it was going west. The wheels in her mind ticked as she set to using her minimal navigation skills and rusty geography to determine where they were.

They spent the afternoon noting the ship's location every hour and using rudimental --- the sun sets in the west and rises in the east -- skills to mark their location on a map. So involved with their task, they nearly forgot to check on Mr. Whyte until they heard a thump and commotion from below deck.

Sarah jumped and stumbled backwards. Angie caught her arm before she fell and together they rushed downstairs. As soon as they opened the cabin door the cat Sarah affectionately named 'Cat' stood at the base of the stairs, his fur standing on edge as if he'd been electrocuted. His back poised as he hissed at something. The bedroom curtain was still open and Bill Whyte lay still on the floor, his chin cocked against the wall and neck stretched.

Sarah, behind Angie, took one cautious step at a time as they walked towards the bedroom.

Sarah grabbed Angie's arm. "Wait!" She grabbed the broom because it was close. "OK."

Angie eyed the broom and continued pacing toward the bedroom. They stood in the doorway staring at Mr. Whyte's motionless body. Angie put her hand over her heart when she realized the pantyhose were still tight around his ankles and wrists. "Honey," she said cautiously as they stepped closer to the bed.

Sarah stood behind her with the handle of the broom raised.

There was no answer.

Angie blinked back her tears as she turned towards Sarah. "What do you think?"

Sarah shook her head. "I think he rolled off the bed." She rested the hair of the broom on the floor and poised her chin on the rounded top of the handle as she stared at him.

Angie twisted her lips. "I guess we should pick him up and lay him back down."

Sarah lowered her brows. "I agree." They stood silently for a few seconds before Sarah suggested, "How should we do this?"

66

"I guess I'll take his arms and you can take his legs?" suggested Angie as she blew a loose strand of hair from her eye.

"OK," she said, leaning the broom against the wall and stepping into the room behind Angie who walked up behind her husband and peered at his face plastered against the wall. "His eyes are closed."

"That's good. That means he's still unconscious."

Angie nodded in agreement then asked, "Can you pull his legs so we can turn him over?"

Sarah tugged at his legs. "He's heavy," she whined, dropping his legs onto the floor.

Angie took one of his legs and together they pulled him until his face was no longer pasted against the wall. It hit the floor with a dull thud. The women walked around behind him, Sarah tugged at his chest while Angie tugged at his legs. An odor of rotten eggs hung in the air followed by a whooshing sound. "Oh," Sarah moaned, crinkling her nose. "I think he crapped."

Angie wrinkled her nose and nodded in agreement as they worked to roll him onto his back. "I'll clean that up in a minute."

In order to get a good grip on him, Sarah leaned over and grabbed the underside of his chest then rolled backwards. As she did, his head snapped to the side and he caught her bare arm in his mouth. "Ouch!" she wailed, hitting his face to free her arm from his tooth hold. Blood dribbled down her arm.

"Oh my god!" yelled Angie as she hit her husband, his eyes wide and staring at her. "Let go!

What are you doing?!" She continued yelling and beating on him until he let go of Sarah's arm. Sarah fell backward and hit the wall, then crawled towards Angie.

"What the heck?!" she screamed holding her arm.

"Let go and let me look," demanded Angie as blood dribbled from beneath Sarah's hand. *Don't panic,* she told herself. "I got this," she told Sarah, forgetting about her husband and taking Sarah's hand, gently guiding her to the kitchen table where she spread out a towel.

Reality hit Sarah as Angie was cleaning and rubbing in copious amounts of antibiotics. "He bit me. I'm going to turn, to change into a dead thing," she said in a shaky voice, tears pooling in her eyes.

"We don't know that," Angie said calmly. "All we know is he bit you, not how the illness spreads."

"I watch the movies and TV shows; once you're bitten that's it. You might as well kill me now!"

Angie narrowed her eyes. "That's a little melodramatic. TV isn't real and neither are the movies. We'll keep an eye on the wound," she said in her mother voice.

Angie turned her head towards her husband who lay on the floor wriggling like a worm towards them.

Chapter Eleven

Back in Spain...

Early morning sunlight streamed in from the top of the window. The area we hadn't blocked off the night before. It was Jack who was unnerved by the monkeys and suggested, since it was almost night, we stay inside the store and leave in the morning. He figured the monkeys would be gone and we'd be able to go straight to the boat. We took precautions and moved all the shelving in front on the windows and doors so nothing could sneak in during the night.

I stretched my legs then noted the firm lap beneath me. Shooting my eyes upwards I watched Bryce's chest heave in and out, his head hung against it. Carefully, trying not to wake him, I lifted myself up.

"Hey," said Bryce.

"Hey, good morning," I responded, dusting my pants off and offering him a hand. He took it and rose to his feet, stretching his long, thin body. My mouth watered a little as I checked out his abs when his shirt rose above his waistline.

I peered towards the shelving, unable to see if the coast was clear. Bryce caught my gaze shift. "Let's check."

We walked toward the windows and peered over a shelf. Beady red-eyed monster monkeys stared straight at me. "Ughh." I let out a large breath, my back sinking against the shelving. "They're still there. What are we going to do?"

"Eat breakfast, then worry about it," Bryce said with a smile as he plucked a pastry off the shelf.

We ate and soon Jack woke up and the three of us ran through various scenarios that included taking our chances, emptying the rifle on the little beasts, only there wasn't enough ammo to kill every monkey. I counted fifteen red-eyed beasts. They discussed taking care of them the same way they did zombies, only the monkeys were much smaller, smarter and faster.

"Maybe we can just make some noise and bring the zombies back," suggested Jack, shrugging.

Bryce stuffed a hand in his pocket as he leaned against a shelf. "That's not a bad idea. In the dream, they wouldn't head onto the beach where the zombies were."

My eyes wide, "How come I hadn't thought of that? That's it!"

Jack glanced at us, a puzzled look on his face as he scratched at his bald head. "I missed something."

"We'll fill you in later. Right now we need to figure out how to attract more zombies from in here," Bryce stated.

"We make noise," I said. "Loud noise."

"The monkeys were loud, but that didn't attract any zombies," said Jack, stuffing the last of his pastry in his mouth.

Why was he the voice of questioning and reason? I thought about it. The monkeys screamed shrilly and piercingly, so maybe it was a frequency that zombies couldn't hear. It made perfect sense to me since I'd already determined they had brain damage. "He's right. We need to make noise, loud noise, but not high pitched."

We knocked down the shelves and beat on them with our weapons, making all sorts of racket. The monkeys started leaping about and cooing at each other in a shrill scream. We continued our noise assault until the monkeys leaped away, replaced by flesh-eating zombies. I smelled them from inside the building, rotting flesh and bones, missing body parts, and their bodies ate up with human bites. Chunks of flesh hung from their mouths. They shuffled towards us and, in the lead, a dark-haired woman running for her life.

The lady's long brown tresses bounced against her back as she sprinted away from the zombies in a purple bikini. Her long legs, dark and muscled, her chest jiggled with each step she took. Bryce was already out the door and slashing zombies as my mouth was still gaping at the sight of the woman. I rushed out behind him and hit my ax into the neck of one deader and then another. Together we spun, kicked, and clobbered each disgusting bag of rotting flesh.

I took a deep breath and held up my hand for Bryce who slapped it, then we walked inside the store where the woman sat drinking bottled water. While we were zombie slashing Jack must have snuck her in. He ogled her perfect model-like body.

She stood. "I was almost past that mob of flesh-eaters when you started making that entire racket.

What were you doing? Trying to get me killed?" she huffed with one hand on her hip. Her accent, I figured, would be Spanish but it wasn`t. It had an English ring to it, making her even sexier.

Bryce spoke up, a look of hurt in his eyes, "We saved your life."

"Because you had to make up for attempting to get me killed!" She sighed. "It's good, I guess, to know there are other lifers out there like me. I haven't seen one in days; not since everyone turned into flesh-eaters and started dining on human flesh and guts. I'm Heather."

"We're sorry we nearly got you killed. We didn't know you were out there, but we need to hurry and get these supplies to our boat before another wave of flesh-eaters comes and finds us." I thought for a minute about her choice of words. She called the uninfected lifers and the zombies flesh-eaters. I like her choice of words but didn't like the way I spied Bryce checking her out.

"Why don't you come with us?" suggested Jack. He was just as bad. *Are all men pervs?*

Oh, great. Let's bring this woman who was every teenage boy's dream. It wasn't her fault, and she was far too old to be interested in Bryce, but the green-eyed monster still stuck its ugly rear in my head, giving me jealous thoughts.

I walked out of the store first, hoping for a stray zombie or two to take my mind off Ms. Gorgeous Heather who I kept seeing Bryce sneaking quick glances at. But the area was empty; no flesh-eaters or monkeys. Behind me were Bryce and Jack as they pulled the loaded cart, followed by Heather. Bryce had given her his shovel and taken my knife.

We ran as fast as possible towards the boat, when *Farmacia* caught my eye -- a pharmacy. "Go on ahead. I'm going in here to get some real drugs, antibiotics and such. With flesh-eating creepers around they might come in handy."

Jack looked at me, puzzled, as if he didn't believe my intentions but Bryce simply nodded and they continued forward.

The pharmacy appeared empty, so I went behind the counter and loaded up on everything. I stuffed a shopping bag to the gills with drugs then was about to slip back over the counter when a whiff of rotten trash made me wrinkle my nose and something grabbed my shirt. I jolted forward and my shirt ripped. Cloth still in the zombie's mouth but, luckily, no flesh. I dropped the bag and swiped my ax towards the zombie. It reeled unsteadily from my quick actions and the ax missed it so I jumped back over the counter, feet first, swinging in the zombie's direction. It knocked him off balance and I smashed the ax into the side of his head just below his ear. Blood spurted everywhere when I pulled my ax out. I guessed I hit the carotid artery.

I left the zombie bleeding out and grabbed my bag, then spotted adult diapers and more feminine products. I stuffed another bag full and exited the store. Ahead I saw them loading the life boat and in the other direction I saw, heard, and smelled a hoard of zombies. They were slow and clumsy so I picked my feet up, clutched the bag, and waved for them to push the boat into the water. Within a couple minutes I was running through the water. It splashed up my legs and soaked my shoes. Heather grabbed the bags and tossed them into the boat while Jack grabbed my hands and pulled me into the boat as the first zombie splashed into the water.

Chapter Twelve

Once the zombies hit water they didn't know what to do. They halted like their legs had sandbags tied to them and snarled at us as we paddled off towards Earnest Earl. Jack then asked, "So what did I miss? The dream thing?"

He had to remember... I glanced at Bryce who gave me a go-ahead nod. "Before the world started turning into zombies, Bryce and I shared a dream that I'm convinced was a premonition. In the dream we were the only two people alive and we took my father's boat after killing a dozen or so zombies. We set sail and ended up on an island we thought was empty but we were wrong, there were red-eyed monkeys who chased us into a pack of zombies. The monkeys wouldn't go near the zombies; that's how we got away."

"Red-eyed monkeys?" said Heather.

I nodded.

"Interesting." Heather smoothed her hands over her legs. "I'm more perplexed by how none of us are infected."

Our eyes shifted from one to the next. That was the question we all wanted an answer to. I tucked the bag of adult diapers beneath me so neither Jack or Heather had a reason to ask about them.

Once onboard Earnest Earl we worked as a team hauling everything onto the boat and finding places to store it. Bryce and Jack handed up supplies as my mom, me, Heather, and Sarah grabbed and stacked everything on the deck. Once everything was stacked we worked on finding homes – food in the kitchen, medicine in the bathroom, and toilet paper and other toiletries in the narrow storage cabinet alongside the wall by the bathroom. We kept the cart too, thinking it may come in handy again.

My mom pulled me aside and into our bedroom once the supplies were put away. "Your dad is awake," she said, pointing towards my father who sat up in bed, fully alert, blinking at us. He made garbled sounds, as a sock was stuffed into his mouth.

"Dad," I said as I stepped towards him. He reached his arms out and my instinct was to rush towards him but my mom put her arm in my way.

"His pulse is strengthening, his breathing is normal, and his temperature is getting warmer. It's almost normal at 89.7 degrees F, but he… he bit Sarah," she said, cringing.

"What?" My eyes narrowed. "She seems fine."

"She is. In fact, the bite is showing signs of healing."

I looked at my father who continued to make gargling sounds with his arms outstretched. His cheeks had color in them again and his eyes weren't glazed anymore.

"I knew something was going on. You've been hiding a zombie on the ship!" hollered Jack from behind us. He stood in the doorway, holding the curtain back. "I thought it was odd all the excuses you made to cover up your father never joining us."

My mom, the voice of panicked reason said, "No Jack, stop," as he walked towards the bed with one hand behind his back. "His pulse is almost normal and look he has color in his cheeks again. I think he's going to be fine."

"I'll judge that for myself," snarled Jack as he approached my father who stared at him with wide, unglazed blue eyes as Jack pulled a knife from behind his back and shoved it at my father.

My father's gargling became desperate as his eyes shifted toward the knife shining in Jack's hand.

I gasped and screamed, "No, not my father!"

He poked the end of the knife at the sock in my father's mouth and flung it across the room.

"Stop Jack!" pleaded my father. Hearing his voice was music. If he was alert, talking normally, with near-normal vital signs, he was healed. Somehow his body had fought off the disease.

Jack staggered backwards in surprise as I lunged for my father, wrapping my arms around him. "Daddy, you're OK!"

"Yes, sweetheart." His eyes scanned my body, sucking in my appearance. No doubt I was covered in splotches of blood and hadn't yet changed my ripped shirt that dropped forward exposing my sides and back. "Now what's going on here?"

The entire crew entered the tiny bedroom. Everyone was so close I heard their hearts beat and felt breath on my neck. They stared at us with quizzical expressions. I sat on the edge of the bed, staring at the group of people who stared back at us, mouths agape. Heather spoke up then, hands on her curvy hips, "I'd like to know too."

My mom spoke up and told the story, starting with how she woke up and he was lying in bed cold beside her, to how he woke up when the meds ran out, bit Sarah and that's when they stuffed the sock in his mouth.

My father looked the most surprised. "I've been tied up in your pantyhose? That's kinky." He waggled his eyebrows at my mom. "For how many days and where are we?"

"Eleven days," Sarah stated matter-of-factly.

Then my mom with her rusty geography and ignoring his man comment, chimed, "Close as we can figure, that's Spain ahead of us and the Rock of Gibraltar to the southeast. We saw a large military ship moving through the channel and followed it with the binoculars until we couldn't see it any longer. It was definitely headed on a southwest trail towards the US."

I knew we were in Spain, but didn't realize that we were so close to Italy.

Heather cleared her throat. "You're all Americans, why are you here?"

Bryce spoke up, his back against the wall, "We're on our way to Naples, Italy to collect my mom and sister."

"And what if they're zombies? Within twenty-four hours everyone in Spain was dead apart from me and maybe there are others, but I didn't see any," said Heather, narrowing her eyes toward Bryce.

"We don't know, but we've come this far. We'll figure it out and, if they're alive, they are coming home with us. And why aren't we sick, and how did my dad's immune system fight off the virus, and how was he infected in the first place?" I spat, the questions rolling from my brain to tongue.

"Norfolk. It's gotta be from Norfolk, Virginia. That's near west from here," announced Jack, running his hand over his shiny bald head.

My dad's eyes shifted to Jack then everyone else. "Can someone untie me?"

Everyone's eyes were pasted on me. My mother and I were beside him and quickly untied him. He immediately stretched his arms and legs. I stood up from the edge of the bed and offered him my hand. He stood, unsteady at first, one arm around my neck while I clutched that hand. After a few steps he was steadier as we walked through the crowd. Everyone moved aside and I brought my dad into the kitchen.

"Are you hungry?" I asked, as if life was normal and my dad hadn't just woken up from some kind of zombie coma, and I hadn't just gone off on everyone.

"Eggs sound good, and toast, but after you've showered. You're a mess," he answered, his voice weak, taking a seat at the table as I grabbed the ingredients.

I smiled sheepishly then gathered fresh clothes. The group had followed us into the main cabin, including Cat who jumped onto Sarah's lap as she fell backwards onto the sofa.

After my shower, Mom joined me in the kitchen and we prepped food. Heather asked where the dishes were and set the table. Bryce and Jack went upstairs and set the boat on course for Naples.

Everyone ate a hearty breakfast of scrambled eggs, sausage, coffee, and orange juice. Sarah cleaned the dishes and Heather looked less physically intimidating in one of my mom's smocks. Her long legs still showed but her curves weren't quite so obvious. She was at least six inches taller than my mom and a bit thinner. My mom had a full figure, but not so full she wore large woman sizes, just enough she had wide hips and a complete chest with a round cheery face and a short bobbed haircut. I looked at myself and wondered when I'd sprout. My face was more oval, like my dad`s, and I wore my straight, light brown hair that was sun-bleached long.

I sat at the table next to Sarah as she rolled up her sleeve and unwrapped the bandage. Grabbing the end of the bandage from her hand, I finished peeling it back and dabbed antiseptic onto it. The blood was dried and it was obviously healing. "I'm sorry, Sarah," I stated, staring at the tooth marks buried into her skin.

"No harm done. It'll heal. He didn't know what he was doing," she said, meeting my gaze and, as if she read my mind, followed up with, "I feel fine."

I nodded as I dabbed on more antibacterial cream, smoothing it in so the wound was swathed in it completely.

Heather took a seat next to us. "Let me take a look," she said. "Odd, he bit you and you're fine. Was his mouth clean when he bit you?"

"I guess. We'd been feeding him water through a tube and he may have had pill residue in his mouth and saliva," answered Sarah.

Heather sucked in her upper lip. "So it doesn't transmit through saliva, maybe other bodily fluids."

Sarah and I stared at her. She smiled. "I'm a doctor in the UK and was in Spain for a holiday."

"Not much of a holiday," Sarah followed up with, her brown eyes sparkling.

Heather chuckled. "No, suppose not. Well, we're still alive." She clucked her tongue. "When the plague hit your area, did you notice anything odd?"

Sarah and I shrugged. "Not really, everything was pretty normal for Florida." Then I remembered my conversation with Bryce right after we found each other. "Since we had a warm winter, the mosquito population was high."

"Nasty, disease carriers, could be. Did you notice any bugs, black and attached?" Heather said, coupling her fingers together and moving them in and out as if to emphasize the together part.

"With little red-heads?" asked Sarah slowly.

"Yes, they fly around everywhere, make quite a nuisance, all stuck together." Heather wrinkled her nose in disgust.

I followed up with, "Lovebugs. But I didn't know they were in Spain or in Britain. They're nasty bugs that are rumored to have been made at a college in Florida to eat mosquitoes and control the population. According to Bryce, whose father is an environmental scientist, they really came from Central and South America to the Southeast US."

"Hmm… There was a mad dash of them before everyone changed. I can't help but blame the little creatures for this plague," Heather said, then stood and left us.

We sat quiet for a second, perplexed. My brain attempted to process how lovebugs made it across the ocean.

Sarah finally broke the silence and my thoughts when she said, "I'm kinda glad you found Heather. It's nice to know there are other people alive in the world. Do you think we'll find Bryce's family?"

"I hope so and I hope they're OK." I picked up the first aid materials when Heather rejoined us.

"Take these every six hours. They're an antiviral." Heather dropped two small pills from one of the medicine bottles I grabbed in Spain.

"How do you know it's viral?" I asked.

"I don't, but as fast as the disease spread it's the only thing that makes sense. You see, viruses are tiny fragments of DNA and they're pretty smart. If one cell won't let them in they'll find another and another until the body has an overwhelming amount of infected cells. They are also tiny and easily spread through air, water, and touch. My bet is this disease is airborne and that's how it made from one continent to the next with such speed," Heather stated in a doctor voice.

"Then why aren't we sick?" Sarah asked, logically, resting her mended arm on the table.

"We're immune. I need to gather medical data from everyone onboard this vessel to determine that one commonality." She smiled at Sarah. "I'm glad you found me too. Now, do you have a notepad I could use?"

"Yeah," I said, jumping up and running into the room I shared with my parents. I came back with the notepad Mom and Sarah used to keep track of my dad's vitals and medication.

Heather flipped it open and read through the data. "Very clever. Whose idea was this?"

I smiled sheepishly. "Mine."

Heather nodded then asked our names and jotted them down on clean pages. "Might as well start with you two."

For the next thirty minutes she asked us all types of questions from medications we'd taken to allergies to any surgeries. My mind was spinning by the time she was through and went on to the next person on the boat.

After dinner, I took a seat at the helm next to Bryce, gazing at his chestnut hair and long, thin body. We'd be nearing Naples by nightfall. At that moment a star streaked the sky and I made a wish.

"Did you see that?" he asked, acknowledging my presence.

"Yup," *and I wished for your family to be somewhere safe, alive, and easy to find,* I thought.

He propped his feet up on the dash to the side of the wheel and tucked an arm behind my back as our eyes glanced toward the darkening sky.

Chapter Thirteen

Morning came too early and butterflies swirled in my gut. The day we'd traveled so far for; finding Bryce's family with no cell phone or any way of communication. Jack coasted the boat into a port filled with ships and boats of various sizes. Tall buildings in various colors, mostly stucco or concrete in construction, towered above the shore, looking as though they would tumble into the sea. My dad took the helm and Bryce and Jack jumped off the boat, weapons at the ready as they tied the Earnest Earl and loaded the tank full with gas. It went smooth and not a zombie or living thing in sight.

I wondered if the virus, well I only assumed it was a virus because that's what made sense to Heather and me, killed everything except cats, monkeys and fish, remembering the one I squished the day after the storm.

Once the tanks were filled I hopped off the boat. Bryce smiled at me. "Glad you're joining us, Zombie Girl," he said in a quiet, almost anxious voice. I imagined this was the day of reckoning for him. The day we traveled across the Atlantic for – to find his family.

My dad took the boat away from the dock and they anchored it far enough into the sea that zombies couldn't reach them. No one figured they swam, especially after how we'd seen them react to water in Spain. His body was still weak from his sickness, but his color was back and he walked and acted human. Hour by hour, he looked and acted more like himself. A couple days of food and rest and he'd be healthy again.

We carefully marched on the docks leading to the solid Earth. Staying quiet, we kept our weapons at the ready. Glancing toward the sky I realized how eerie it truly was, not a single bird or bug flew or swarmed over head. The message it sent was contradictory; the sun was bright as it beat on our heads, yet the dead silence was spooky like a horror movie -- except it was my life. It was completely silent and had been silent for days. The only other life we'd seen was the darn monkeys. *Did the virus kill everything?*

We followed Bryce, who halted once we reached the parking lot. There were a few cars which meant a few deaders somewhere. "It'll be easier and safer if we can jack a car," he said.

"We don't have keys. Does anyone know how to hotwire?" asked Jack, holding the rifle over his shoulder.

We looked towards each other, everyone's eye shifting from one to another.

"I can figure it out. It's just a couple wires." Bryce neared a little gray car. He held his hand against the window and peered inside. It was empty, so he tried the door. It was locked. We split up and peered into other cars trying the doors. I lifted the handle on a little white car and felt something squishy beneath my finger. I snatched my hand back and eyed my finger. A black bug in the shape of a V hung against my middle finger. I flicked it and it fell to the ground, a tiny red dot head caught my eye. I studied it further and determined it was a lovebug, but how did it get here?

Running to the front of the car, I knelt down and checked the grill. The nasty bugs always stuck to grills and destroyed paint when they splattered against it. They were a huge nuisance every spring and fall. To my dismay, but not surprise, several more lovebugs were smashed against the grill. *Disgusting!*

I lifted up and blew out a breath then moved onto the next vehicle and studied the grill, then moved around the car, keeping my eyes on the hood and side of the car, then the door handle – more lovebugs. When my eyes shifted to the window, two glassy brown eyes stared into oblivion somewhere beyond me. My breath caught with surprise and I took a step backwards.

"Jack found one, c'mon." I turned and saw Bryce heading past me. The zombie continued to stare blankly and it brought its hands to the window and pawed. I stumbled after Bryce, following him to the car.

So far, so good. We'd been quiet enough not to attract unwanted, dead, stinky company. The one in the car didn't seem to notice us. Bryce saddled himself under the dash, his legs stretched outside the car as we stood guard. The area stayed clear and deadly silent until we heard the sound of the motor roar. We piled in the little car and Bryce took off just as the *drip drag* shuffle of zombies came for us. Still too far away and not walking too fast, we didn't fear them or stop.

"You know where you're going?" asked Jack.

"A little. I've been here several times," Bryce said as he whipped the little car to the right onto what I assumed was the Italian equivalent of a freeway. Bryce dodged cars stopped in the middle of the road. A zombie or two or three pawed at the glass windows in their cars as we swept past them. We followed it for quite some time, passing clusters of tall, colorful buildings. It felt as though we were heading straight into the heart of the city. He took an exit and made a right onto a road filled with old buildings jutting from the ground. My heart thumped inside my chest as I thought of what a cluster the area was and how many deaders must be close by.

Soon the area became less populated, as if we were now on the outskirts of Naples. Instead of colorful buildings that looked glued together and close enough to have a discussion with a neighbor through any window, they had space and small yards.

Bryce made another turn. "Oh crap!" said Jack as Bryce slammed on the brakes. I jolted forward, then slammed backwards into the seat. In front of us was a car wreck blocking the road, and several zombies milling about. Bryce reversed the car back to the other road and sped on ahead. The zombies followed us, but as we sped away, I could no longer see them. That hoard wouldn't catch us in time as they stiff-walked, rigor setting into their joints.

He made the next turn. The road clear, he sped over it, made a right then another left back onto the zombie-blocked road. When they heard the car they turned around. Not agile, they moved one leg at a time, teetering like broken ballerinas until they faced us then walked towards us, but the car was simply too fast.

We followed this road for a while before he turned onto another road and parked in front of a white two story house with a red concrete-looking roof, many flowering shrubs surrounding it. "This is it," he said, but the lack of confidence in his voice alerted me. Something wasn't right.

"You're sure?" I asked. Jack peered at him as we both waited for his response.

"Yes." It was a reluctant response and I guessed his apprehension hinged on what we'd find inside -- his family safe and healthy, or the alternative.

"Then what's wrong?" I questioned, leaning forward and resting my hands between the front seats.

Bryce shook his head. "It's nothing. I... am just used to this street being busy -- people walking, gardening, kids playing. It's empty."

I nodded. It was eerily quiet and vacant. We exited the car and walked towards the house, unsure what we'd find inside. The door was locked.

"There's a back door," said Bryce as he followed a path around the house toward a gate, his shovel propped high and ready. We took careful footsteps to not make any noise and alert any deaders that might be hanging around. The stench of death was in the air, so they weren't far. I hoped they were stuck inside their homes.

Bryce tried the back door, it was locked too. He shrugged and turned towards us as we stood behind him. "Anyone know how to pick a lock?"

A bang thudded against the window behind Bryce. My eyes shot towards it and were glued to the dead lady planted against it. A huge chunk of flesh from her cheek was missing, exposing her teeth and tongue. Dried blood covered most of the rest of her face.

Bryce's mouth dropped and I sent silent prayers that it wasn't his mom. Jack pulled back the safety on the rifle and fired. The shell whizzed straight through the window and into the woman's skull. She dropped like a sack of bricks.

Bryce's eyes widened and he wore a horrified look on his face.

"That wasn't your mom, was it?" Jack stated with a grimace.

"No, that was my aunt, and you just alerted the zombies to our whereabouts. Thanks," he said in a sarcastic tone.

"Jeez, they know we're here. We might as well break the rest of the glass and get inside," I said, clearing the glass away with my ax and pounding out the rest so we had a space clear enough to crawl through. "Lift me up."

Jack walked beneath the window, brushing alongside a flowery shrub, and lowered his back for me to stand on and climb inside the house. I didn't see any more zombies, so I jumped off the side of the counter that was beneath the window, landing on both feet only a few inches from Bryce's dead aunt. My mind played de dant, de dant over and over. As kids we used to kill ants and say, 'deddant, deddant,' to mean dead ant. Over time it became de dant. I chuckled as I thought of how twisted my mind was to think of it at such a time.

"Help," urged a quiet female voice. I stopped and listened, but heard silence. *Did I really hear a voice?* Most likely it was my imagination.

"Unlock the door, they're coming!" shouted Jack as they beat on the door. I opened it and moved to the side, they both stumbled inside, nearly toppling over each other. Several zombies were stumbling towards us, no more than fifteen feet away.

"Help," came the voice again. I couldn't make out what direction it was coming from, or if it was an adult or someone younger, like my age. It definitely wasn't a small child.

Bryce caught his balance and stared at me. "Was that you?"

"No. You heard it too?"

He nodded. I locked the door and stayed at the window to fend off any zombies who may be agile enough to try and climb through the window, while Bryce and Jack set off through the house.

I heard doors opening and their footsteps echoing over the tiled floors downstairs, then one of them went upstairs. I listened with my eyes peeled towards the window. The first set of zombie fingers rested on the edge of the windowsill. The nails were dirty, covered in a conglomerate of blood and possibly flesh particles. I whacked them with the shovel but they didn't move and no scream followed. As hard as I hit any living thing would feel the pain, so zombies didn't feel anything. I felt awkwardly comforted knowing that slaying them didn't hurt.

I took a different approach and used Bryce's dead aunt as a stepping stool then grabbed a kitchen knife resting in a holder near me to cut the fingers off. I forced the knife onto the fingers and peered into the dead eyes of their owner and pushed downward. The glassy dead eyes stared at me but held no recognition of pain.

Peering down at the sausage appendages, they lay lifeless on the countertop. That answered a question; limbs didn't survive without their host. A sudden shaking caught me off guard and I stumbled off his dead aunt, falling backward into the refrigerator. The handle jabbing my back. "Ouch!" I screamed.

The shaking only lasted a few seconds. As a Floridian, the earth didn't shake there, so moving ground was an entirely new concept to me but not completely foreign. I'd learned all about earthquakes in junior high and spent several months watching the news nightly with my parents. I just didn't know Italy had them -- Japan, California, but Italy?

A commotion upstairs caught my attention; something fell hard against the floor. Curiosity made me leave my post as I scrambled to the stairs. "Everyone alright?" I screamed.

"Yes," came Jack's response, then his bald head peered down at me. "We found another but Bryce took care of him."

"OK," I said returning to my post. No more zombie fingers clung to the edge of the window. I let out a large breath and that's when I heard voices, one clearly a woman's. I hoped it was his mom as I waited, staring around the room. The kitchen was small and block shaped. An entryway separated it from the next room. The house was old and not open and airy like Florida homes.

Deep growling caught my attention and I shifted my gaze to the window. A set of dead brown eyes stared at me. This one was tall. I took the shovel and poked it right into its face, shoving it backwards. It stumbled, then fell backwards and I lost sight of it.

Within a few moments Jack entered the room. "We found them. They're OK."

"Oh, good," I stated, shoving the pointy end into the zombie's face as he reappeared at the window. Again he fell backwards, now with two shovel marks across his face. "We need to board this up or get out now," I added.

Jack nodded and left me alone in the kitchen. It felt like forever, but was about fifteen minutes, before Bryce and Jack appeared with a nightstand. They hefted it onto the kitchen counter which was wide enough to hold it. By its construction, and the obvious strength it took them to lift it, I assumed it was solid wood.

"Come on," said Bryce as he took my hand.

The next room, which I hadn't noticed earlier, was decorated with modern furnishings that didn't fit the style of house. A woman with chestnut hair and green eyes sat on a green chair, holding a little chestnut-headed girl in her lap -- Bryce's mother and sister.

"Mom, this is Maddie." He turned towards me. "Maddie, this is my mom, Katrina, and my sister, Melissa."

We nodded to one another, then Katrina spoke, "There's a car beside the house. The keys are in the kitchen in the top drawer beside the sink." I hadn't noticed a car earlier and assumed it must be on the opposite side of the house from the path we took.

I didn't understand why, if there's a car, they didn't escape the house, but figured it was better to wonder at the moment than discuss anything. We needed to get back to the boat, so I traipsed to the kitchen, opened the drawer, and found the keys.

I marched back into the room and Bryce was gone. "How long has it been since…?" my voice drifted off as Katrina's eyes filled with tears.

She sniffled. "Three days. It happened so quickly. In hours, my sister and brother-in-law changed. I managed to lock us in the extra bedroom we'd been sleeping in."

Well that answered my question. She was obviously too terrified or in shock to think of escaping. "You must be starved and thirsty." We couldn't set out with weak people; any number of things could happen.

She nodded.

I went back into the kitchen and opened the fridge. I decided packaged drinks were safer, remembering what Heather said about viruses spreading. There was a bottle of unopened juice, so I placed it on the counter, then rummaged through the cabinets until I found two glasses and a box of some kind of wafers. I brought them out and poured them each something to drink.

Bryce was back with a suitcase. He rested it beside a door I hadn't noticed earlier. It must be the front door.

Melissa raised her head from the comfort of her mom's bosom and took the drink. She drank the warm juice heartily and snacked on the wafers. No sooner did they swallow the food than the earth shook again -- stronger than the last. The walls of the house moaned as they rattled at their joints. I braced my feet and leaned forward to catch my fall. Objects dropped from the walls and a loud crash echoed from the kitchen.

Chapter Fourteen

When the rumbling shook, I sprinted into the kitchen with Bryce. The dresser had fallen directly on top of his dead aunt. Jack rushed in after us as we all lifted it back up, placing it in front of the open window. The stench of death was strong in the air.

"What was that?" I asked.

"An earthquake," Bryce said with a hint of anxiety in his voice. "We need to leave." He walked into the living room area and looked at his mom. "How long have these earthquakes been happening?"

"It's Naples, they happen often enough, but have been more frequent the past couple days," she responded.

What did Naples have to do with earthquakes? Oh my gosh! It hit me; earthquakes caused by volcanoes. Italy was famous for having an active volcano, Mt. Vesuvius. *But just how close were we?*

"We need to get out of here. You ready, Zombie Girl?" asked Jack as he grabbed the rifle he'd rested alongside the coffee table but had fallen onto the floor.

"How close are we?" I asked, cringing.

Katrina spoke, "Too close. The base is only a few miles away." The contortion of her face was a perfect match to the horror of her words.

Oh great! If zombies weren't enough, a volcano was going to explode and turn us into human ashes. I headed towards the door, ax in hand. It was time to escape this zombie, volcano infested nightmare of Italy and welcome the safety of Earnest Earl.

Bryce and Jack behind me, we opened the door, weapons ready for slaying, but nothing stood in our way. The zombies were too stupid and all bunched in the back of the house. The car we took was directly in front of us within twenty feet, and the other vehicle was around the side of the house. I pointed straight ahead but Bryce shook his head as he clung close to the house and peeked around the corner.

Starting up that car would certainly capture the zombies' attention. I didn't get it; the other car was so close we could all make a run for it and pack inside before the zombies had a chance to get to us. Bryce disappeared around the corner, then I heard a car door and a motor revving. Within a few seconds a large SUV-type vehicle backed from the driveway, drove across the sidewalk, and parked in front of the door, followed by the *drip drag* shuffle of zombies. I jumped into the back along with Jack, as Bryce held the door open for his mom and sister.

They scrambled inside the vehicle as the putrid death smell that accompanied the deaders first wafted into my nostrils. This vehicle was far roomier and, although it was a bigger risk, offered more in the way of comfort than the tiny vehicle Bryce hotwired.

Bryce stepped on the gas once his mom and sister were safe inside and the SUV bounced off the sidewalk and into a zombie stumbling towards us from the street. He fell against the hood, then dropped to the ground as the vehicle bounced over him, making crunching and squishing sounds just like in the dream when I ran them over with my mom's car.

Bryce's sister Melissa said, "Eww," and curled her body tight. She couldn't be older than four judging by her size and the fact that she wasn't yet in school.

We sped off, leaving the zombies behind, and headed back into the city. A few stragglers stumbled around, but no one who looked alive.

"Are we going to see Daddy?" Melissa asked in complete innocence. She seemed a little more comforted and less an appendage of her mother now that we were clearly moving away from danger, or maybe it was comfort in being surrounded by living people and seeing her big brother.

"Yes, when we get back to the US," answered Katrina in a strong voice that surprised me.

I was thankful they were both OK and healthy, and felt more comfort myself the closer we got to the port.

"I'm so glad you showed up. I've been worried. We lost radio and cell phone reception days ago. Before we lost TV there were horrible reports all over the country and from other countries. But you made it," Katrina beamed to Bryce.

He nodded as he maneuvered the vehicle around a couple deaders wandering in the road. One was a topless woman whose skirt sagged around her hips. I wondered where her shirt went. The other was a teenager. Her hair stuck out everywhere and bites covered her arms. As we passed, her blank glassy blue eyes stared at me, more like through me. I closed mine, unable to look into her soulless body.

The SUV bounced over something in the road. From the back seat, I wasn't sure what, except it didn't crunch like a zombie. A wheezing sound caught my attention as the vehicle swerved and Bryce stepped on the brakes.

"We got a flat. I hope there's a spare," Bryce stated as he looked at his mom.

"I believe so. Jack," who was sitting in the passenger seat, "open the glove box and press the red button. It'll release the hatch."

Jack's eyes shifted as he scanned the area, then popped the hatch. He and Bryce stepped out of the vehicle and gently shut their doors. We were somewhere in the heart of the city, surrounded by buildings that most likely held dead people.

"Everyone needs to get out," Bryce said after he lifted the hatch, "except you, Melissa."

I slid out the back, with my ax ready as I circled the SUV. It lifted off the ground as Jack loosened the lug nuts. Bryce joined me as we kept vigilant watch over the area. A breeze blew my ponytail over my face and the unmistakable smell of rotting flesh swept up my nose. They were close.

Jack tightened the last of the lug nuts and he gently let the SUV down. Melissa's head peered over the backseat with a delighted look in her eye. I'm sure sitting in a vehicle that moved up and down was a game for someone her age.

Jack and Bryce lifted the gear back into the rear, while his mother slid into the back seat with her daughter. I stared ahead in between buildings as dozens or more zombies shuffled towards us. *We need grenades to kill that many*, I thought as I slipped into the back seat next to Melissa who was oblivious to the danger surrounding us.

Bryce, Jack, and Katrina were aware right along with me just how much danger we were in, as their eyes shifted to the masses now out of the shadows of the alleys between the buildings. Bryce stepped on the gas and the ground beneath us rumbled. The road moved in waves as fierce as those in the ocean during the storm.

Chapter Fifteen

Bryce didn't stop. He guided the vehicle over the asphalt waves as they lunged us forward. The zombies toppled onto each other. The road appeared as though it was going to swallow us, then a large rift opened up in front of the vehicle. Bryce slammed on the brakes and turned the vehicle sideways. Its wheels stopped just short of the rift.

"What do we do?" asked Katrina with a shudder in her voice.

"We walk it," stated Jack.

I knew we weren't far from the port, but the odds didn't look too good for us surviving as I glanced at the wall of zombies picking themselves up from the ground behind us.

Bryce nodded. "We don't walk it. We run it," he said, opening his door and scurrying around the vehicle. He helped his mother out, then he collected Melissa in his arms and swung her onto his shoulders. I handed him his shovel and we ran, all of us, in the opposite direction of the zombies.

Gray smoke and soft ash littered the ground as we pushed forward, leaving the zombies in the dust. They didn't move fast enough, but the volcano may blow its top anytime and that we couldn't outrun.

After a few blocks Jack paused, hands on his knees. "I'm tired. I need a rest." The sun would be setting soon, as golds and violets streaked the sky.

"There isn't time!" demanded Bryce.

"We can't leave him here and he's not the only one who needs a break," said Katrina, backing him up. "The dead things are behind us. Why don't we try a building? Maybe we can all rest for a bit."

Bryce looked around. We were surrounded by brightly colored buildings. He tried a door and it was unlocked. "I'm going in first with Jack. Zombie Girl, you have to watch my family."

His eyes pleaded with me and I knew he entrusted the job to me because he trusted and knew I was a teenage killing machine. I nodded and tucked us into a corner between attached buildings. I stayed in front while we waited for the all clear.

Several minutes passed, maybe fifteen, when I heard a shuffle. I put my hand to my mouth and looked at Melissa. She copied me. No more than five feet from us a zombie shuffled past alone, its rancid odor making us all crinkle our noses. Melissa plugged her nose with chubby hands. She was adorable and I was glad that I stood in her way so she didn't see the nasty sight as it hobbled away, a gaping hole in its back uncovered by its torn shirt. It never took notice of us. When it was a clear, ten feet past us, Bryce opened the door and waved us in. We padded inside, careful to be quiet -- my eyes on the zombie the entire time. It never turned its head.

Light streaming from the large windows gave us enough to see. We were inside a clothing store. Bryce led us through the aisles to a break room area. It had a table and a couple couches and two doors. One he closed behind us.

I didn't ask in front of Melissa, but figured they decapitated a few zombies judging by the time it took them then carefully stuffed them away somewhere. "What's behind the other door?" I whispered in Jack's ear.

He smiled devilishly. "A bathroom. Don't worry its cleared."

Ah, well I guess they'd found a deader inside it. "Good," I said as I walked towards the door. My bladder was ready to be emptied.

When I came back out everyone else took their turn and we rummaged through the cabinets for any kind of snack food. We put our scavengings together and had a couple bottles of water, three candy bars, and a bag of more wafers. Bryce divvied it up and we ate and rested. I imagined the air outside dark. It was too bad that I was stuck inside a building with flesh-eating zombies outside and a volcano threatening whatever was left of our existence to enjoy the sunset in another country.

To amuse ourselves and make everything feel "normalish" for Melissa's sake we played silly games like twenty questions and Simon Says. She chuckled and giggled when it was her turn to be Simon, Bryce purposely made mistakes. It was a side of Bryce I hadn't yet seen and it made him even more drool-worthy as I saw how carefully he interacted with her.

A worn-out Melissa fell asleep on a couch, Katrina petting her hair. When she was fast asleep, evidenced by her tiny snore, we snuck to the other side of the room and huddled together. "We're not far from the port but we don't have a vehicle and I didn't see one anywhere nearby," whispered Bryce.

"When we were outside waiting, one walked by us, we stayed quiet and it never knew we were there," offered Katrina as she pushed her hair behind her ears.

She was right. It didn't notice us. So maybe it didn't see or smell. The one I chopped the fingers off of never cried out in pain. None of them did as they went down. Maybe the only sense they had was sound. I'd looked into many of their eyes but never had one actually acknowledged they saw me. Their eyes stared dead ahead "They can't see or smell or feel pain. They can only hear sound."

"We don't know that," said Jack with narrowed eyes.

"Sure we do. Think about every encounter you've had with one of them. They look through us with hollow eyes, they feel no pain when we kill them, but sounds always capture their attention," I said proudly.

"So we just walk past them. We don't run," offered his mother with a smile.

I smiled back. Leave it to the women to figure it out.

"Is everyone forgetting Mt. Vesuvius is revving to blow?" said a disgruntled Jack with his hands and eyebrows raised. "Even if what you say is true of the zombies, can we outrun an unpredictable volcano?"

We all shrugged. There was nothing to say. If the zombies didn't eat us, we'd be barbecued right along with them. It was night now. There was no electricity to run street lights and plenty of flesh-eaters. We were doomed.

Katrina snuggled beside her daughter, Jack on the other couch, and Bryce and I settled on the floor. We were younger and more agile, so we gave the older folks the more comfortable spots. Really, it was forced seniority. That didn't make the floor any less hard, but Bryce's shoulder was soft when I rested my head on it. In turn, he rested his head on mine and eventually we dozed off.

In my dream I was riding a roller coaster that fell off the tracks. The car with me in it flew high into the air and I screamed at the top of my lungs as it suddenly plummeted to Earth. I popped my eyes open, the floor rolled around me, Bryce was holding me tight while Katrina held onto her daughter with one hand and the edge of the couch they were on with the other. Jack was balled under the table.

"We need to get back to the boat. That volcano is going to blow anytime. I'd rather take my chances with the zombies than become human toast," I said, rising and grabbing my ax. I kicked the rifle at Jack, tossed the shovel at Bryce and threw nothing at Katrina and Melissa. There was nothing left to toss; we'd even left their luggage in the SUV. Then I remembered the knife in my pocket. The stiff object pressing against my butt almost felt normal.

I walked up to Katrina as she pulled herself off the couch. "Take this," I said, handing her the knife.

Her eyes widened and she stuttered.

"We need every able bodied person." I lowered my voice and whispered in her ear, "Shove it in their head or brainstem at the base of their neck."

She wrinkled up her face but took the knife. Bryce and Jack waited by the door. Opening it slowly, Bryce ventured into the hallway and walked towards the light streaming in from the windows. There were no other doorways in the hall so we were relatively safe.

Katrina leaned down and whispered, "Stay very quiet," to Melissa, who put a finger to her lips.

Once we got into the main room, we moved through the aisles toward the door. The windows were large enough to see nothing waited for us outside. I stepped in front of Bryce, leaving him in the middle with his family and Jack in the back with the rifle.

Particles of smoke and ash fell around us in a light dusting. Bryce ripped the bottom of his shirt. I grabbed it from behind, taking it out of his hands and tearing it at the seam, then handed him the new rag. He wrapped it around his sister's face and tied it in the back to keep as much volcanic debris as possible out of her airways. The rest of us pulled our shirts over our faces and stepped quietly away from the building and towards the sea.

We walked through alleyways, staying off the main road, dodging trash, careful not to make a sound. Mixed with the ash, I smelled the salty air, knowing we were close. My heart thumped as I couldn't wait to get back on the ship. I wondered how my family fared the night and how Sarah's bite was healing. It was a good thing we found Heather, as she was a doctor. That gave me a little solace that they were OK.

I halted at the edge of the alleyway as I had been doing since we started our trek. I peeked around the corners, making sure the area was clear. So far we'd only come across one deader who was wandering down the street. We waited a few minutes then carefully walked across the street to the next alley. It never noticed us so maybe my quick-thought hypothesis about them only hearing sound was true -- a heck of a way to prove it.

I poked my head around the corner, spotting four zombies milling about -- two women, a man, and a child. My heart sank as I saw the little girl, no bigger than Melissa, walking aimlessly. Her skirt dirty with blood and a string of flesh hanging from her closed mouth. Her hair was matted with more blood. I quickly pulled my head back and sank against the wall.

Bryce mouthed, "Zombies," without making a sound.

I nodded and mouthed, "Little girl."

He crunched his face in dismay and shot a glance at Jack. I don't know what he mouthed, but within the next minute he was at my side. He winked at me, held out three fingers, then two, then one. We ran out into the open and slayed the adults easily. We both glanced at the girl who snarled at us as she staggered our direction. I cringed, it was my turn. He'd killed the teen zombie we found in Spain, now I had to kill the baby. I threw my ax into her neck and she toppled backwards, the ax ripping her flesh as she fell. My breath caught in my chest and I tried not to think about what I did. There wasn't an option.

We walked back to the alley and saw another zombie moving towards the alleyway. It must have heard us. Bryce jumped into action, running toward it with his shovel and clopping it on the head. A set of arms reached for him, then another. I grabbed his sister's hand and looked at his mom, "We need to go now!"

"What about Bryce?" his mother said through tears as his shovel came down on another and Jack ran to assist him.

We didn't have time for this. His sister was small and I wasn't killing another zombie baby, not today anyways. I could see the port ahead and feel the sea's breeze whipping my ponytail. Without a second thought, I picked up Melissa with my free hand, holding my handy dandy ax in the other, and ran. She wrapped her little arms around my neck and her legs around my waist. I didn't look back. Bryce wouldn't want anything to happen to the precious little girl who plastered herself against me.

When we reached the marina, I set her down and swung my arms above my head to alert my dad. The sun shone directly in my eyes and I couldn't see the boat, but I heard the motor catch as little Melissa clung to my leg.

"Mattie, Mattie," she said. I glanced down at her and followed her pointer finger. Staggering towards us were three zombies. I covered her eyes as I prayed for my dad to hurry. The zombies moved closer and I didn't want to kill them in front of Melissa's innocent eyes.

Spray washed up the side of my body. I turned my head and my mom held out her arms within a foot or so of me.

There wasn't time for words as I lifted Melissa. "Grab onto my mom," I shouted, using all my strength to toss the girl to my mother who caught her in the middle. She stumbled backwards, Melissa falling on top of her. I nearly lost my balance and dropped into the sea. Catching my balance, I saw my mother stand, Melissa buried in her shoulder.

The earth rumbled beneath my feet and groaned in dismay, so I braced my hands on the ground beneath me. When it stopped, I used the advantage of agility and ran towards the zombies wobbling on their unsteady feet. A shot rang out and brain matter and blood sprayed from a zombie's head, the sound echoing in my ears. When the zombie dropped, I saw Jack behind it with Katrina and Bryce on his tail and a whole bunch of zombies.

The boat sputtered as my dad pulled into a dock and called for me.

"Not yet, not until everyone is onboard!" I screamed. He narrowed his eyes in dismay. I knew that look. Now that his health was back, I was his little girl not Zombie Girl, killer of the dead.

Heather appeared on the deck and one by one helped everyone onto the boat. I slashed at bloodied zombies, watching as they dropped and moving to the next until I felt my body being pulled back and a familiar voice in my ear, "Stop, Maddie, everyone is safe."

He dragged my body onto the boat and I turned, wrapping my arms around my father's neck. Zombies dropped off the dock and fell into the water, instantly sinking.

"I love you, Daddy," I whispered as he pulled me even closer.

"I love you too, Maddie." I felt his warm breath on my head and it was a good feeling.

Chapter Sixteen

The boat coasted toward the Strait of Gibraltar, the sun setting once again as Bryce leaned against the side of the boat next to me. "It's really pretty," he said. His fresh clean scent moved through my nose with the gentle breeze. At some point I'd stopped worrying about being covered in blood, but at the moment it felt good to be clean and even better to be standing next to a clean hunk.

"Yes, it is."

"Thank you for what you did today." Our eyes met and he leaned down, his nose touching mine, his warm minty breath against my face. Our lips touched and a loud, low grumble surrounded us on all sides -- the spell of the moment broken. Our heightened senses kicked in. "The volcano," we said in unison.

Rushing onto the top deck, we joined my father and together watched a huge gray plume of smoke, several miles wide and high, billow into the atmosphere. It hung there several seconds or several minutes, I don't recall how long, until it finally dropped. Volcanic bombs splashed into the water, some within a football field of us, and smoke and ash snowed around us. Through the blackening sky a flow of brilliant red lava shone through, oozing down the mountain towards Naples. No doubt covering it as it flowed into the sea.

We watched, mouths agape, before I realized Jack, Heather, my mom, and Sarah had joined us.

110

Their eyes wide and mouths hung open as we watched in horror, completely helpless.

My dad suddenly spun into action and cranked the motor; moving at full throttle wasn't enough. The strait wasn't getting any closer. The Rock of Gibraltar seemed to mock us as our boat was sucked backwards, never getting any closer. The motor worked to keep us stationary for several minutes.

As quickly as the entire scenario began, our boat was lifted possibly fifty to sixty feet into the air, wobbling on top of the tsunami wave as it dropped and lunged us headlong. Water rushed forward, covering us and running off the top deck. A popping sound crashed in my ear as one of the masts broke off, dropping onto Jack and rushing off the boat with the receding water. My heart dropped as the wave let us go and we fell downward. We grabbed onto anything within a hand's reach. Our screams were loud enough to wake the sleeping dead and energize the living dead. Earnest Earl rode the wave that sent us spiraling towards a landmass.

Once the sea retreated, it deposited us on the top of a cliff where we skidded over the rocky area. Popping and cracking noises filled my ears. I imagined chunks of boat ripping off the side and holes in the bottom with the thrashing Earnest Earl received. We were all going to die as the boat careened, bumped, and jumped down the cliff.

We clung for life as our bodies were tossed around like rag dolls. My grip around the rail tight as a bump tossed my body sideways and threw me over the edge, my legs dangling over the cabin. I dropped,

111

landing on my butt onto the deck and rolled over lying flat on my stomach until the boat came to a sudden stop with a crash that sounded as if the boat was breaking into pieces. I opened my eyes, not realizing I'd closed them, and uncringed my face. The deck was still in one piece beneath me.

Carefully I picked myself up, sure the boat wasn't moving anymore, and went down into the cabin to a teary eyed Melissa and a freaked out Katrina. Both seemed OK, other than scared and horrified. I didn't see any obvious wounds or broken bones, but was sure they were bruised, same as me. At the moment I felt no pain as adrenaline pumped through my veins like a car on the Autobahn.

Within minutes, I heard voices around us, outside on the deck, and the cabin door opened. A frantic Bryce rushed down the steps past me and to his mother and sister. The three held each other in a long hug before they asked about broken bones and bruises.

I left the cabin and went outside. Ash and dust hung in the air. The boat was wedged between two huge natural rock structures. I jumped off and my mother rushed to me with a hobble. She wrapped her arms tight around me.

"Are you OK, honey?" she asked, eyeing me up and down.

"I'm fine, Mom, but your leg..."

"I think it's a sprain. It'll be fine."

"Let me take a look," I said as I helped her down and knelt beside her, rolling up her pants leg.

It was already swelling. "Can you wiggle your toes, move your ankle?"

"Yes," she cringed from the pain.

I looked for Heather and spotted her with Bryce, helping Katrina and Melissa off the boat. I called for my father. "Dad, Dad."

"He's looking at the damage to the boat," my mother responded, holding her leg.

I walked towards Heather who was tickling Melissa. Her tears were dry as she giggled. "When you're done, can you look at my mom's leg?"

"Certainly. I'll be right there."

I continued towards the boat and found my dad on the other side, gawking at the massive hole in the bow. His gaze shifted when he saw me. "We're lucky you know," he held his arm out and wrapped it around me. Now that I stared at the boat, we were lucky. It seemed impossible to look at this pile of fiberglass and believe we all walked away. Most of it was still intact, but it would never be seaworthy again.

After Heather had the chance to check on everyone it seemed the only major wounds we incurred, besides the bruises I knew would be all over our bodies in the morning and the ache that would follow, was my mom's sprained ankle and the deep cut across Jack's head above his right ear. Heather fixed him up with the supplies we had and wrapped a covering over his head. I noted then she had a large, two to three inch gash on her arm. It was no longer bleeding, but someone had to care for the doctor.

Heather finished wrapping Jack's head and took a long breath. She stretched out her legs, a solid rock structure beneath her, and gazed toward the sky. I sat next to her. She'd cared for and looked at everyone, but no one asked about her. I put my hand on hers and she turned her head and looked at me. "Would you like a water?"

"Oh, yes. Thank you." She opened the bottle and took a long swallow. "That definitely tastes good."

"You have a large gash on your arm," I stated, grabbing the antiseptic and a cloth.

She twisted her arm and glanced over her shoulder. "So I do."

I dumped the antiseptic onto the cloth and dabbed at her arm. The dried blood soaked into the cloth.

"Rub a bit of this on it," she said, handing me a tube of something with Spanish writing on it. I knew popular words, not pharmaceutical names. They didn't teach that in Spanish class. I gently rubbed the ointment in. When I finished, she put her arm around me and tilted her head against mine. "You're a brave girl, Maddie."

Chapter Seventeen

Shook up, in shock, dazed, but in relatively good health, we stared at each other through the ashy air as we surveyed our surroundings. Below us was the sea, only tiny waves hitting the shoreline now as I gazed downward. Around us on the other side was solid rock and mountains. Our plan, whatever it was, now vanished. We were beached like a whale and staying on the boat wasn't an option.

Sadness clutched my gut as I glanced again at Earnest Earl. We wouldn't be able to take extra clothes, just weapons and food supplies. We made a circle as we decided what to do next. My dad spoke first, "Earnie's not taking us anywhere but we have enough food to last for a bit. I suggest we get down the cliff, maybe we can find another boat."

"We can't head down that cliff, how do you suggest we get down there?" offered Jack.

"We're not going anywhere tonight. It will be completely dark soon. The air is filled with volcanic ash and I'd rather fight flesh-eaters when I can see them. And that little girl needs a good night's sleep," voiced Heather. The little green monster had completely moved on and I loved Heather's logic and medical prowess.

"You're one hundred percent right. We'll eat, get a good night's sleep, and figure it out in the morning. Whatever we do, we do it as a group," said my father, his eyes taking in the mountainous terrain.

The boat was lodged solid between rocks. It literally wasn't going anywhere. Bryce started a fire with a few chunks of wood from somewhere on Earnest Earl. I was glad he remembered his Boy Scout skill, and we warmed up beans and wieners and had a cup of canned fruit each. It wasn't gourmet, but it was food, and tasted great after eating wafers and candy for dinner last night.

Katrina tucked Melissa in for the night. She was a great little trooper who hadn't complained once since we collected them in Naples. The only fear I'd seen in her was after the tsunami. Naples seemed like ages ago as I considered the path ahead of us. If we had climbing gear we could most likely reach the shoreline below, but it looked rocky not sandy so we'd have to take the high road through the mountains. I was far more worried about the treacheries of climbing around unknown plants and the possibility of wildlife such as leopards and bears than I was about zombies stuck on the mountain top.

Maybe we'd get lucky and find an abandoned vehicle somewhere. I hoped so for Melissa's sake. She was too darn small to be mountain climbing. The boat was tipped a bit, but not much. I could snuggle onto my trundle for the night. The hole in the bow was large enough for something to climb through, so we wedged whatever we could into it. My parents slept in the bed above me; Katrina, Melissa, and Bryce in the other bedroom, and Jack and Heather in the living room. It was tight but we were out of the raining ash. Maybe this was nature's way of telling us we needed a bigger boat.

As I dozed in and out of sleep I thought of all the zombies in Naples covered in drying, hot lava. Their bodies melted, nothing left except bones. Or possibly those were melted too. The volcano continued to rumble but didn't erupt again. If it did, I figured we were high enough it wouldn't affect us. The ash from the eruption still spilled into the air, falling like a light snow dusting.

"We-yak," screamed a man as he chased me through wetland marshes at home, my legs splashing into the water beneath me. "We-yak," he screamed again, closer this time. I was suddenly on an airboat coasting through the marshes – nasty lovebugs splatting against the boat and my face. I wiped them out of my eyes then put on goggles conveniently placed in front of me. "We-yak!" he screamed as I bolted upright in bed.

It took a minute for me to get my bearings and the dream lingered as if it meant something. *We-yak* that's what Bryce's father said after he turned, but Bryce hadn't a clue what it meant, if anything. Something inside told me we had to get back to Florida, back to his father. Maybe Bryce's mom would know what *we-yak* meant. *Did she know about her husband?* Life was becoming a nightmarish blur, but I was sure I remembered Bryce mentioning that he told his mother about him turning. I brushed chunks of hair from my face and lay back down. It was still dark outside.

The smell of powdered eggs and toast grabbed my attention and urged me awake. My parents had already vacated our little sleeping quarters. I sat up in bed. My entire body screamed at me as pain radiated throughout it. I pushed it aside and padded gingerly into the living area and it was empty, so was the other bedroom, meaning everyone was outside. I glanced at the little bathroom and wondered if it was safe to use for a tinkle. Shrugging. It didn't matter, we were leaving the boat, so I took my tinkle in the toilet then joined everyone outside.

They all sat around the campfire and shoved food into their faces. It might be the last decent meal we had for a while. I joined them after we suited up to take on the mountain; nine tiny living people and a cat against whatever horrors awaited us.

We geared up; Jack with the rifle, Bryce with the shovel, and my dad with a heavy wrench and heavy-duty bolt cutters. We had enough bats that Bryce used extra clothing to rig carriers on our backs for weapons, extra shovels as well as a bottle of water each and a couple flashlights. Heather donned a medical kit and hoe -- I assumed so she wouldn't have to get close to anything. My mother had some type of gardening tool that doubled as a walking stick and weapon. Sarah wore a jacket she tucked Cat into, his head popped out the top and a fireplace poker. Everybody carried at least one weapon, except little Melissa. Jack pulled the cart we stole from Spain loaded with food. I wasn't sure how well it would fare in the terrain, but respected the idea.

In a pack, we headed over the mountains. We went downhill as much as we went uphill. It was silent, like everywhere else, and we each moved slowly as our bodies were past sore. There was nothing moving, we were isolated with no GPS. I did stuff my phone and charger into my pocket in case. It hadn't done me any good for days but seemed a waste to leave behind.

For what felt like hours, we walked and my body loosened up and the pain lessened. Bryce or I carried Melissa when she grew tired. Finally we stopped when we made it to a tree line. The vegetation wasn't thick, but offered shade.

"It's about noon," my mother announced, shading her hand over her eyes as she peered at the ashen sky.

We put together a small lunch and rested. Katrina sat with Melissa who sucked the juice out of a can of fruit she just finished. I thought to ask her about *we-yak* but thought better of it. I'd wait until we were someplace relatively safe.

"I'm guessing we're somewhere in Africa," announced Jack, stuffing a bite of tuna sandwich into his mouth.

"How do you figure?" asked my father.

Jack swallowed then answered, "The tsunami washed us somewhere high, into mountains but we could see the sea below us. The Atlas range extends over the northern region of Africa."

That made sense. I left them to their discussion and snuck next to Heather. "Any ideas on the virus yet?"

119

"Well, we have a larger crew now, so after I speak with them I'll have to reevaluate."

"But you had an idea?"

"Sort of, but the pieces don't all fit so I'm at a bit of a loss to say anything yet." She smiled. "If we can get back to civilization and find a medical office of some kind where I can take blood samples and such I may be able to come up with a working hypothesis."

I nodded.

She clucked her tongue. "You say you're allergic to mosquitoes."

"Yeah," I answered, looking at my nails. I'd put on a fresh coat of bug repellant nail polish after my shower yesterday and made sure to bring the bottle with me. I didn't need to turn into a watermelon while we were wandering through the mountains with only Heather for medical care.

"Did you know Bryce is allergic too? In fact, we all are to varying degrees. That's what causes the red welts and itching."

Did I know? It didn't seem like news, so he must have told me sometime in the past. Then I remembered he wore bug repellant bands over his upper arm. I glanced at him and, sure enough, he had one visible beneath his sleeve. *Did our allergy mean something?*

"Looks like it's time to leave," she said, pushing off the ground to her feet.

Everyone was rising; our little pit-stop was over. We hadn't walked more than fifty feet when Jack halted in front of me. I almost ran into his back. "Do you hear that?" he asked.

We all stood stock still and listened. Water; it was rushing water.

"It's water," said Bryce as he leaned his ear to hear where it was coming from. "We should follow it."

Oh no, déjà vu. I remembered the dream and the watering hole we found. That's when the red-eyed monkeys discovered us and chased us smack into the zombies. Taking in a deep breath and watching my step, I followed Bryce and everyone else toward the sound of rushing water.

It was possibly thirty minutes to an hour later we found the source of water and followed it. Since water runs downhill it made sense, but I cringed at finding any type of civilization because that meant finding more zombies.

It was far too thin to be a river, so I figured it was a stream which would eventually lead to a river. The sky was changing shades of color again, meaning sundown was near. We'd need a place to rest for the night. The stream grew wider and the land around us leveled. I lifted my father's binoculars that hung around my neck, placed them in front of my eyes, scanned the area, and spotted a dot of brown on the horizon. I continued watching the dot grow larger as we moved forward.

It wasn't a dot at all but a wooden house, along a wide area in the stream. I moved close to Bryce and handed him the binoculars to make sure I wasn't hallucinating an oasis on the horizon. "Follow my finger," I said as he'd said to me in the past.

Sarah trotted alongside us. "What is it?"

"A house, maybe a ranger station," said Bryce, lowering the binoculars and handing them to Sarah.

By this time we'd gotten the adults' attention as they stopped moving and stared at us, my dad wearing his tell-me face.

"A house, where the stream gets wider," I said.

We made plans to take over the house for the night. The zombie fighting men would go in first. I offered to go in as well but my dad gave me a firm 'no'. Bryce made me feel better when he told me he'd rather I was watching his family than Jack.

The house was still and quiet, which really didn't mean anything, and a large shed or small barn was a few yards behind it. It sat flush with the ground, no porch, and the wood looked more than a little weathered but the structure was solid. Us women plastered ourselves flush with the house as the testosterone flaming men went inside.

The house was in a clearing surrounded by woods on the opposite side from the stream. We stood still and a small rustling sound caught my attention. At first, I thought it came from inside, but when it happened again I realized it wasn't from inside the cabin but the woods, only fifteen feet or so from where we stood.

Chapter Eighteen

Tan furry legs stood close, too close, when I saw they were attached to a lion. Out of the corner of my eyes I glanced at Sarah, Cat still snuggled against her chest, next to me and Katrina beside her. Melissa was sandwiched between them and Heather and my mom stood closest the door. I shifted my eyes back and it was still there.

My heart thumped hard enough to jump outside my chest, but I stayed still and quiet. The lion was lying, his head on the ground like a puppy, watching the house. I didn't know if it saw us, but I sure saw it and he was huge. His mane was matted and hung loose around his thick neck.

I focused my attention toward the men inside and listened as I kept one eye on the lion. My ax wouldn't do much to hurt him unless I was close, but in that case I'd already be dead. He was bound to be far more clever and faster than the deaders.

Scuffles sounded from inside the cabin and a door opened, then the door closed and footsteps moved closer to us, then further away. The smell of death carried past us with a breeze. I figured the guys were cleaning up since they killed a zombie or a zombie was close. I kept my eyes and ears peeled and heard and saw nothing. The lion scrunched his nose and whipped it about then moved a few steps backwards. I guess he didn't like *eau de zombie* either. I hoped they were going to let us in soon. It had to be safer than outside where we'd soon be lion food.

The door opened and Jack motioned us in. I put one hand out over Sarah and Melissa and put my other finger over my mouth. Melissa looked up at me and put her finger over her mouth like it was a game. Heather, Katrina, and my mom gave me odd looks but got the message and slid along the wall, staying quiet. One by one we slipped inside the cabin. I kept one eye on the lion. When it was my turn, I grabbed the cart and wheeled it inside with me. It made so much noise I was pretty sure if the lion wasn't aware of us before it was now.

"Mommy, I have to potty," urged Melissa and she wriggled on her feet.

"All clear," said my father.

While Katrina and Melissa were in the bathroom I pulled everyone together. "I didn't want to say anything outside, but we aren't alone."

"Zombies?" asked mom.

"No, furrier, smarter, faster. A lion."

"You're serious?" asked Jack, lifting his brows, causing forehead wrinkles that webbed onto his bald head.

"Yes."

"Holy crap, I thought they were extinct here. A lion. Really?"

How did he know so much about lions? "Maybe zombies took over the "Pride Lands,"" I quoted *Lion King*, "and he was searching for food."

Jack gave a half chuckle.

Katrina and Melissa returned after a few minutes and Katrina, noticing us all in a huddle, knew something was up and raised a brow. We split up and set up our camp for the night. There were blankets, so Sarah, me, and Bryce made mats for everyone to lie on. My mom, who enjoyed cooking, got to work on a meal with Katrina's help and Heather played games with Melissa. We all avoided the elephant in the room, or rather, the lion.

The cabin was one large room and a bathroom but it had running water. The décor was light with a single family picture on the wall of an older man and woman. "Were they here when you entered?" I asked Bryce, pointing at the picture.

"We had to kill him, but she was already gone. Her legs were eaten and most of her torso."

"Zombie dead or *dead dead*?" I questioned with narrowed eyes.

"*Dead dead.*"

"Was her head intact?"

"Yeah," he answered, raking his hand through his hair. "So people... can die without... becoming zombies." As the words formulated on his tongue the same idea formulated in my head.

"Where are they now?"

"We dragged them outside."

I figured that because of the sudden stench after I heard a door open, whilst I was plastered to the house stressing over the lion.

I grabbed his hand and pulled Heather aside, then jabbed him in the ribs to tell the story.

"Ouch!" he grumbled as he rubbed his ribs, "no need to be so violent." He told her what he told me and she pulled the notebook I'd given her out of her homemade knapsack and wrote something down, then she asked him more questions about the woman's color, anything he noticed about her.

She continued to jot things down then asked him to show her the body. He guided her to a curtain beside the back door that led to the other building and pulled it aside. She wrinkled her nose. "Eww."

After, she returned to Melissa and continued playing silly hand games. Cat crawled between them and sat beneath their clapping hands. Every so often he'd put a paw upward as if trying to play too.

We soon sat and ate dinner, then a tired Melissa stretched her arms and Katrina set about primping her for bed. It amazed me how she made it seem so normal when nothing was normal.

I snuggled next to my dad who was sitting on one of the homemade-looking chairs with a plush butt cushion and wrapped an arm around his neck. "Do you remember anything about when you...?" my voice trailed off.

"I remember the marina and getting onboard Earnest Earl," he quivered slightly at the mention of his dead boat. "Then I remember going to sleep and waking up tied with a sock in my mouth. It was like I lost all those days. The feeling is like losing time during surgery."

I'd never had surgery, so couldn't completely relate. "We kept you full of muscle relaxers."

He wrapped both arms around me. "Whatever you and Mom did, I'm grateful. I'm not a zombie and get to live the rest of my life and enjoy each day

126

no matter how much a struggle. I'm alive and I owe it to my family."

I kissed his cheek and rested my head against his. Life was crazy and undefined but we still had each other and the ability to love and live each day and person to the fullest.

Once Melissa was fast asleep with Cat curled next to her, Katrina sat next to Bryce. I listened to their conversation. "So what happened earlier? When everyone was huddled together?"

He shifted a bit then said, "We have a tiny problem."

"And?!" she demanded.

"Maddie saw a lion outside the cabin."

"A what?!" her voice beamed.

"Quiet, Mom, Melissa's asleep."

She leaned her head against the wall behind her and sighed. I left them to their moment and sat next to Sarah on the mat she'd made as a bed. "It looks like you have competition," I said, pointing to Cat and Melissa.

She smiled. "I do. I think that Cat helps keep the both of us sane. Everything is so crazy. What was it like twenty days ago we were regular freshmen with fifteen-year-olds' problems? Today we're like survivors."

"How's your arm?"

She put her arm in front of us and twisted it slightly. "Mostly healed."

The smaller teeth marks were gone and only a couple raised bumps remained where his front teeth did the most damage, but in time they'd heal as well.

"I'm pretty sure we've been on three continents in the past couple weeks time," I chuckled. That sounds so strange.

She giggled. "When you put it that way." As soon as the words left her mouth, millions of pings tapped against the roof.

Rain; it was rain. We leaned against each other and fell asleep. Tomorrow was a new day.

Over the next the day the rain continued, the sky black with a combination of thick dark clouds and volcanic ash. While the volcano continued to smolder, ash and dust accumulated in the atmosphere that now mingled with the rain, making clay-like splotches in the dirt.

My mom made full use of the kitchen and the food supplies we'd dragged with us. She fried spam and made biscuits. The stove was gas, so she was able to bake.

Since the rain continued to pour in buckets, it was decided we wouldn't go anywhere until it stopped and the ground dried. The clay splotches were probably slippery as well and since we were all sore and bruised still since the tsunami we mostly lay around and rested our bodies, taking the time to heal.

On the second day, in our boredom, Sarah and I went through the drawers. Inside we found a map that neither of us could read since it was written in a foreign language, but we understood the universal parts. The cabin was located near a road that led to a bigger road that went over the mountain. There were towns located along the road but none near us. We were truly in the middle of nowhere. Nonetheless, the discovery of the map was good news.

Curiosity drove me toward the shed behind us. The ground still very wet, I didn't venture outside toward it, but made a plan that when it was dry enough, and I wouldn't sink into the mud, I'd explore it. Who knows what kind of treasures might be inside it?

On the third day before the rain stopped, Bryce discovered the wooden bench opened up. Inside was a gold mine. Two small guns and a sniper rifle along with ammunition but nothing to fit the shotgun -- errr…rifle -- the big gun Jack was partial to. I was beginning to wonder if the dead owners were survivalists of some kind. We all smiled with the luck and fortune, then tore the little cabin apart searching for more treasures, but didn't find anything.

A map and more weaponry put us in a good spot and I considered we may be able to stay in the cabin for some time. Feeling comfortable and safe, but not complacent, I decided to bring up the *we-yak* conversation with Katrina.

She eyed me curiously and said, "It doesn't sound familiar. I've never heard that term, but I'll continue to play with it." We were nowhere with its meaning. I thanked her and joined Sarah and Cat playing with Melissa.

By the fourth day, the rain stopped, and by the fifth day the ground was dryish. Everyone still sleeping, I sneaked to the back window and moved the curtain back. The bodies lay about halfway between the cabin and shed. They had dark curly hair and their skin was ashy white, partly because of the clay drops covering them. I imagined, when alive, they had darker skin – tannish maybe.

I carefully crawled through the mats and tapped on Bryce. His green eyes opened and stared into mine. He lifted up on his elbows while I pointed towards the window and mouthed, "Shed."

He arose without making a sound and crawled with me to the back door. I grabbed my ax from our weapon piles that we kept on shelves near the door. I handed him one of the guns as he lifted the heavy wooden board that locked the door. Together we traipsed outside.

"Cover me and I'll head towards the shed," he whispered, taking a step away from me.

I grabbed his arm. "You cover me with the gun. If the lion is anywhere near you can shoot him."

He nodded as I took careful steps towards the shed, keeping my eyes on the woods. Bryce's eyes darted around as he kept watch -- the bodies a few feet from me now, I slipped on a muddy splotch and lost my balance. I pushed my hands out in front of me to break my fall and heard rustling in the woods. By the time I looked up, the lion stood a few feet away, his eyes staring into mine. Not dead and staring beyond or through me, but right at me.

Bryce had the gun raised, but I put my hand up. The lion hadn't moved closer and, if science class was right, male lions have manes and don't usually hunt, nor do they usually seek humans for a meal. I glanced at his body and it was thin, meaning he hadn't eaten in a while. I didn't want to be his first meal in days. My racing heart slowed a little and I steadied my breathing as I lifted up.

Bryce moved away from the house, keeping the gun on the lion. One slow step at a time, he moved toward me. The lion shifted his eyes towards Bryce. The three of us stood there for several seconds before I moved closer to the dead people. The lion wiggled his nose and shook his head as if disgusted.

That gave me an idea. He reacted the same the day I first saw him, when they dragged the bodies outside. I took another step towards the dead people and another. The man was closest to me, his legs within my reach and lower than the rest of his body as they were resting in a deep groove. The lion watched but didn't move so I swung my ax hard and cut off a chunk of leg. It surprised me how easily the ax went through the dead zombie man. The lion shifted his eyes towards Bryce and stepped closer to him.

I cringed and picked up the jellified zombie leg chunk. It oozed over my hand and I gagged as I tossed it towards Bryce. The lion backed up more. I chopped more pieces and threw them towards the shed, towards Bryce, and at the lion. He shrunk back and retreated to the woods.

I waved Bryce towards me and we rushed to the shed. As we reached it, I realized it had a padlock on, so I swung my ax with force and the lock dropped away. I pushed the door open, not aware of what may be on the other side and not caring as we rushed inside and threw the door closed.

Surrounding us were walls of tools and pelts of various sorts. I spotted a sink and ran towards it, letting the cool water wash the zombie gook off my hands and ax. Strips of meat or homemade jerky hung from the ceiling and in the middle was a van. The wheels were large like it was made for the mountains. Our eyes met and smiles covered our faces.

Before we checked out the van, we searched every nook and cranny of the shed to make sure we were alone, and that's when I heard my father's voice: "Maddie, Bryce."

"We've been discovered," I said, walking towards the door. Bryce followed and we opened it. My dad gave us his what-the-heck-are-you-doing face and I slipped him a crooked guilty face smile.

"See what we found," Bryce shouted, "and stay close to the body parts."

My father lifted his brows but followed Bryce's instructions and kept his steps beside our trail of arm and leg chunks. "What's that all about?" he asked when we closed the door behind him.

I shrugged. "Encounters of the lion kind. He doesn't like the smell of dead zombie."

My father nodded in dismay, then he eyed the van, "Does it run?"

"We don't know yet, but there's a set of keys hanging on the wall over there." Bryce pointed.

"Let's give it a try." My father opened the van door and peeked inside. "It's clear." He climbed onto the driver's seat and Bryce handed him the key.

He cranked the motor and it caught. "It's about time luck was on our side." He smiled.

Back inside the cabin we announced to everyone about our treasure and made plans to leave -- a map, a vehicle, and plenty of weapons.

Chapter Nineteen

There's a second exit out of the shed and a manmade dirt road. Bryce, my father, and I decided to take the van and the map and explore a little before we took our entire little village away from safety. We loaded up with weapons just in case -- it's a dangerous world -- and brought the map to guide us.

The manmade dirt road was slow going, mostly because my dad was easy on the gas as it bounced along. Potholes and slippery areas mottled the road. I watched out the window looking for life. If lions, monkeys and fish were out there, maybe other animals were too, but I didn't see any, just lots of trees.

At the end of the road, it turned onto another road that was in better repair and my dad pushed the van a bit faster. We passed more trees and a cry like the sound of a baby wail broke the silence. My eyes darted into the woods and my dad slowed the vehicle. Our eyes searched the woods and sky around us.

Instead of getting out we continued, our eyes peeled, and shifting to every noise in the woods. The wail cut through the air again and my dad pulled over. "Maddie, stay in the car. I mean it."

"Dad, I was fighting zombies when you were incapacitated," that sounded far more mature than 'tied up'. "I can handle it!"

"Fine, stay close to us. We don't split up."

134

I rolled my eyes as he turned towards the door and opened it so he wouldn't see. Once we got out of the van, we gathered in the front and followed where the sound seemed to come from. Stalking through the woods they were silent, not a leaf rustle or crack of wood. Then somewhere above our heads the wail screamed, blasting through my eardrums.

I shifted my eyes upward and spotted the source. A large, black bird with strange dark feathers that stood on end like a bad Mohawk on its head, and a sleek, long crimson beak. *A zombie bird?*

The long beak and size made me immediately think 'carnivore'. Its eyes followed us as we stepped backwards toward the van. A slight breeze carried the rancid odor I recognized all too well. I turned on my heels to head to the van and came face to face with the first zombie I'd seen in days.

His glassy eyes stared through me and his clothes were covered in dirt but was otherwise physically in one piece. If I hadn't seen his face and recognized the jerky movement of his body as he stepped closer to me I'd have thought he was still among the living. Without a second thought, I threw my ax hard into his neck and yanked it out; blood spurted everywhere.

Someone grabbed my hand and pulled me towards the van. I glanced at my father beside me, then glanced to my other side and spotted Bryce. We climbed back into the van and my dad cranked the motor and pressed the gas. The van kicked up dirt and we were back on the road.

The events sifted through my head. The lion didn't like the zombies. The monkeys don't like the zombies, and the ugly bird hollered. *Was it warning us? Were all the animals warning us, or looking for safety?* I kept my thoughts to myself.

Maybe another half hour down the road, the trees became less dense and my dad pulled over. We were on top of a peak of sorts and could see the vast ocean. Getting out of the van, my father walked forward. Bryce and I exchanged glances then followed him.

Our eyes fixed on what he saw. A huge ship -- like a naval ship -- was sailing on a direct course to us. Remembering what Jack said about our location, I twisted my head, observing what I could. To my left was a rock I used to orient myself, the Rock of Gibraltar, making the strait below us and the Atlantic in front of us.

"What do you think it means" I asked.

Bryce and my father glanced at me and my dad said, "I don't know, except we aren't alone."

We stood there, a slight breeze blowing against our faces, and watched. My stomach twisted in horror and dread instead of the happiness and joy I should have felt. By the looks and stances of my father and Bryce I assumed they felt the same as me.

"We need to get back," said Bryce, shifting nervously.

The adults had a pow wow when we returned. I listened as they attempted to keep their voices low and heard comments ranging from 'we're saved' to 'maybe they're responsible for the zombies'. They

finally decided on keeping an eye on the
whereabouts of the Navy and observing from afar
until we had a better idea what was happening.
Siding with caution was always wise, and I was
growing more and more curious by the minute.

Bryce sat on his mat studying the map. I
dropped down beside him and whispered in his ear,
"I say we wake up early and take the van. We can
spy easy, just the two of us."

A sly smile erupted across Bryce's face.
"Sometimes I think you read my mind."

Maybe I did. We did share a dream that started
this whole thing.

The following morning, armed with binoculars,
the map, the compass around my neck, and my
trusty ax, I slipped out the door with Bryce. He
carried the sniper rifle, his shovel, and a flashlight.
Quiet as snakes, we left the cabin and scurried to the
shed, following our zombie body part trail even
though the lion was nowhere in sight. Bryce lifted
the heavy wooden beam locking the door and rushed
back to the van. Once we were both settled and he'd
cranked the motor, the shed front door creaked
open. My breath caught, then I spotted a plume of
dark ringlets pulled into a high ponytail move
through the door – Sarah.

In her hand was a shovel. She opened the side
van door and climbed inside. "I'm coming with. You
guys get all the excitement."

She was right. So far she'd stayed behind on all
our missions, but not this time. She leaned against
the front seats and put her hand out. We smiled,

exchanged glances, and I put my hand over hers and Bryce topped our hand pyramid.

"Let's do this," she said, filled with excitement that I guessed was mixed with anxiety.

Since we knew the way, it didn't take long, and we followed the road further so we were above the large military boat. Bryce turned off the road and pulled the van into the trees and we stole across the street. The dry mountain air chilled my skin. We walked for a bit, my eyes and ears on high alert as I knew we weren't alone. Five or six yards from the van we found a spot between two high rocks and cowered between them. The ground between was like hardened clay from the dried volcanic dust. When I squatted, it cracked from the force of my feet. I propped my head above the rock in front of me and focused the binoculars on the military ship beneath us. Bryce did much the same thing with the rifle.

The deck of the ship looked like a runway with a pad on each side. Several helicopters were parked on the deck and soldiers milled about as though they were preparing the flight deck and copters for take-off. In the middle of the deck was a large structure I assumed was a control tower of sorts used for steering, navigation, communication, and anything else. On top of it was a panel-like object that moved, maybe it was radar or communication. I didn't really know. On the side of the tower structure were the words *Beware of Jet Blast and Motors,* next to that was a giant 6.

Along the side of the ship were the combination of letters that said *LHA 6* and further down *USS America*. This was definitely a US carrier and, as large as it was it was, was much smaller than I expected a carrier to be, at least the ones I'd seen before. As a Floridian from Jacksonville, I'd seen my share of carriers. I'd have to ask Jack about it. As a former Coast Guard he should know. My own parents weren't military. My mom worked at a bank as a loan officer and my father sold *smart phones*.

A stream of soldiers, possibly fifty, exited the ship; over their faces were gas masks, and covering their bodies was bulky camouflage and boots on their feet. Over their heads they wore helmets. They rushed off the boat using a large ladder-like structure, carrying large rifles in their hands and into the city below.

"I think that's Casablanca," said Sarah. The map was spread out before her. I glanced where she pointed. The map showed the city off the Atlantic and the ports below.

I jumped as gunfire rang through the air and into my ears. They fired their large rifles in short bursts and zombies were dropping to the ground. This went on for thirty minutes or so, becoming less and less. We all watched in near horror. At the same time, I admired the efficiency. It was a faster, less messy process. Hundreds, scratch that, thousands of zombies littered the ground in piles.

Within another thirty minutes or so Sarah, the binoculars pasted to her eyes, asked, "That looks like the same ship we saw exiting the Strait of Gibraltar and heading towards the US. What are they doing?"

Without binoculars I couldn't make out well what was happening below, but Bryce answered her question. "Those people are healthy, like us."

Sarah handed me the binoculars and I watched. My mouth dropped when I saw the soldiers forcing people onboard the ship. Many people went willingly, but some bucked and struggled, not wanting to leave their homes. My mouth dropped. *What would they do to us if they found us?*

From beneath the boat, vehicles that looked similar to tanks emerged and sped through the water. On the deck the helicopters whirred into action and, one by one, lifted off the deck, moving in different directions over the land.

I gulped and we swapped glances. "Get down and stay put," said Bryce as he lay over us.

"Can you breathe Sarah?" I asked in all seriousness.

"Yeah," she squeaked. "Really, Bryce?"

"I'm wearing gray. Your pink shirt and Maddie's red one makes you stick out like beacons."

I hadn't thought of that. "Why do you think they're taking the survivors?"

"Because they're alive, testing maybe. The Navy gets their orders from the government," he said.

"I'm glad we aren't the only ones alive. They must have dragged fifty people onto the ship. Instead of hiding, maybe we should go with them," Sarah said as she shifted beneath Bryce.

I wasn't sure about that. I didn't believe the military or government was out to get us, but I wasn't sure about going with them. We'd come so far on our own and my mission wasn't over. Right now, there were no rules for us, and I wasn't giving that up, not yet. "How long are we staying like this?"

Bryce lifted up. "I don't hear or see the copters. Quick, let's get across the street."

The sun was high overhead, beaming against our heads and backs. The ash cloud lowered the temperature a few degrees and, I hoped, marred the helicopter pilot's vision. We slipped across the street and into the woods for cover. Once we reached the van we slipped inside and regrouped. If we headed back now, the van would be a sitting duck for the helicopters. The vehicles with big guns that exited the bottom of the ship Bryce said were amphibious and would drive up on land.

Obviously their mission was to kill zombies and take the survivors. If the Navy was operating, that meant we had some semblance of government in the US. The location of our country, the Pacific and Asia to the West, and Europe and Africa to the East, Central and South America below us, and Canada above gave us the perfect location to send out these kill and capture missions. Not to mention we had the military resources. Unable to see their faces under the masks, I wondered if the soldiers were all from the US or if other countries were involved and how many.

"I think they still have communications and are possibly responsible for blocking radio, TV, and cell for everyone else," voiced Sarah. "They had that obvious radar or whatever moving on the top of the tower and if they're on missions they need communication. These are trained soldiers not mercenaries."

She had a good point that we all agreed with. Bursts of gunshots and the whirring of helicopters went on and off all afternoon. We cowered together inside the van as world war 3 raged around us. I wondered how our families were.

Then a cracking of twigs grabbed all our attention. "Lie flat," I whispered, tossing a thick blanket that was bunched up behind the seat. There were windows on both sides, not to mention the ones on the back doors. The metal floor beneath us was cold, it made the heat from the blanket bearable. We lay flat as the noise grew closer; definitely footsteps.

"Not much dust on this, hasn't been here long," said a muffled observant male voice.

"Try the door," said a female voice with a southern US accent, possibly Georgian. Through the gas mask, it was difficult to be sure.

The driver's door rattled. My heart pounded against my chest. I felt Bryce's beside me. We lay still and quiet as all the doors were tried, the only sound was our hearts and I felt their breath against me as heat.

I was so glad we'd locked all the doors. "Doors are locked."

Static buzzed like from a walkie-talkie or radio. BZZZ-SHHH "10-19."

Squawk, BZZ, "Roger that," the male responded.

"Probably belonged to that group we found earlier," the female voice announced.

Group? Not our group. Urgency rippled through my body and anxiety rolled in my gut at the thought of them finding our little group and there was nothing I could do about it until morning.

Once we heard their footsteps walking away from the vehicle, we threw the blanket off and drew in large gulps of air.

"Do you think they found the cabin?" said a near hysterical Sarah with wide brown eyes.

"No, they couldn't. Everyone is safe," Bryce said, his voice wasn't convincing but the words calmed Sarah.

"We need to get out of here and I'm sure the adult units are really pissed," I urged with wide eyes.

"They're gonna have to be pissed. We don't know how many others are wandering around and it's growing dark," barked Bryce.

"He's right. If we leave before sundown they might see us if they're still out there. If we leave once the sun sets we risk them seeing the lights on the van. Either way, we're stuck until morning." Sarah leaned back against the interior paneling of the van.

A couple hours passed and darkness fell. We exited the van, creeping back to our spot under the cover of night, the moon in the sky only a sliver, so it was especially dark.

The helicopters were back and a skeleton crew of two guys on the flight deck, guns in their hands. The lower deck, where the amphibious vehicles exited, was closed. After about thirty minutes of no action we decided to go down and check it out.

Climbing down the mountain was easier when we thought about it than it actually was. The rocks helped us keep our footing and from slipping, but we should have chosen the road which was longer. My hands, arms, and legs wouldn't be so full of scratches.

Once we got into the city, we noticed the piles of dead bodies. They were neatly tossed every couple blocks. The number of dead far outweighed the living. It was more than creepy walking in the dark amongst dead zombies.

"That's so gross," Sarah cringed as she walked the long way around a pile of dead zombies.

"I like them better dead this way than trying to eat me," chuckled Bryce.

I had to agree. They were far more pliant lying in piles. "And they stunk just as bad before."

"Yeah, well, I thought the military cleaned up its messes?"

"There's a lot more of them than military, Sarah."

She shrugged. "Guess so."

Vehicles were all pushed aside, so we walked in the middle of the road staying away from the zombie piles. I glanced inside the stores and buildings, trying to envision the city filled with life instead of death. A communication store of some kind caught my eye. The soldiers used walkie-talkies. "Look," I pointed.

Sarah squinted her eyes, then it clicked. "Gear."

I smiled and Bryce suggested, "On the way back. Good catch, Zombie Girl." He lifted his hand for a bump.

We moved closer to the docks but away from the USS America. The soldiers had big guns and plenty of lights. There were several yachts docked nearby so we padded quietly as if we were sneaking out the window for a rendezvous and tried a fifty to sixty-footer docked between the mass of boats. It wasn't the biggest or the smallest.

The door wasn't locked, more it was kicked in. As a group we checked each room. We had one flashlight between us and kept it low. As we cleared each room we also closed the window coverings. Once the boat was cleared, we sat down in the spacious living room. It was an open plan and merged with the kitchen which was much larger than the kitchen nook in Earnest Earl and the refrigerator was still cold and packed with food and the cabinets were stocked.

There was a total of four bedrooms, two baths, and even a washer/dryer unit. The yacht had two floors and the steering and navigation had its own room inside. Relaxing on the large comfy sectional, we each opened a soda and a bag of chips.

The cabin door creaked and we froze, then it was silent. We glanced to each other and the next thing a creak groaned from the floor and the barrel of a gun was staring us down.

Chapter Twenty

Holding the gun was a boy with short dark hair, almond shaped chocolate eyes that shifted towards the sniper rifle Bryce had laid on the coffee table in front of us. He didn't look more than fourteen. The gun shook in his hands and my body shook in fear, but not at having a gun pointed in my face. I was Zombie Girl and had faced one treacherous event after the next. His shaking hand against the trigger was the cause of my fear.

On the other hand, it was comical and I forced my chuckle down when I realized the safety was still on. He looked ridiculous in blue and orange striped pants that stopped a clear two inches above his ankles and, to make it worse, he wore sliders and had the oddest-shaped large toe. It resembled the state of Texas on a map and the rest of his toes were long and skinny like twigs. He was better off wearing shoes to cover his hideous feet but, then again, would his large toe fit?

"What are you doing here?!" he demanded in a loud whisper and an English accent that was mixed with something I didn't recognize, North African maybe.

I spoke up, trying to appeal to his humanity and keep my laughter under wraps. At this point, I didn't know how long he'd been on his own. "We're like you, survivors. We aren't here to hurt you or take you."

146

"How do I know this?" he said, waving the gun in my face.

I lost it then and burst into laughter, followed by Sarah. Bryce cleared his throat and kept a straight face. "Because we're the same age. We found this place and thought maybe we could get some rest," he answered. The boy was more scared than ready to shoot us.

"You're Americans. What are you doing here? Did you come with the ship?"

"Do we look…like…military," I said between giggles.

"You have a gun pointed in your face and you mock and laugh. What is so funny?" he asked, his face crunched in anger and rage.

"You can't shoot with the safety on," I spat, controlling my giggles.

"You need some better pants too and sliders don't go with that outfit, nothing goes with that outfit," Sarah said, sniffling from laughter.

He looked down. "What's wrong with these pants?"

At that moment Bryce could no longer stifle his amusement and it came forth in an almost belly chuckle.

The boy stared at us as waves of laughter erupted from us until our sides hurt and tears poured from our eyes.

The boy's eyes softened and his chest shook then his whole body as he joined our laughter, the gun still in his hand. After several minutes our laughter subsided and he cleared his throat. "I like these pants. They aren't in style in America?" His expression serious, we all busted up again, finally stopping when we couldn't anymore due to pain in our sides.

I wiped my eyes. "We came by boat but it was washed ashore after the tsunami. We only learned about the military ship, same as you."

He laid the gun beside the rifle on the table. "Where have you been staying and how come they didn't find you?"

I swallowed and opened my mouth to speak but Bryce beat me to it. "In a cabin in the mountains. We saw the ship and wanted to know more about it so we left and hid in an abandoned vehicle. They almost found us."

"Is your country. Why not go with them?"

I sighed. "Because we don't know what they're doing, why they're doing it, and we've survived on our own. We come from ground zero, where this strange illness began."

After that he opened up and we learned his name was Bennet and his mom was Moroccan and his father British. They flew in from the UK and were visiting family. He'd been on his own, hiding out, slashing zombies and scavenging when and where he could, hence his horrible attire. His family turned several days ago. He was lucky to get away. He'd found others and they watched each other's backs until today when they were taken. He'd hidden by staying one step ahead of the soldiers and, running in here after they cleared it, he figured it would be safe.

We told him about our group and offered to bring him with us. I remembered the soldiers' words and hoped our group was still there. He declined but said to meet him here after the soldiers left. He didn't know how to power or drive the boat and offered it to us. The ignition key dangled in his hand.

"How do we know that's the key?" asked Bryce.

"Follow me, I'll show you," he answered, shuffling past us.

Leary that it was a trick, but without much other option, we followed him. There were more of us so it was gutsy on his behalf and he posed little threat to us.

When we got to the bridge, he put in the key and turned it far enough to display a navigation panel that lit up. "Convinced now?" he asked with a cocky smile.

We nodded and Bryce answered, "It's time for us to get back, we have a long ways to go. We'll be back when the soldiers leave."

He nodded and followed us to the cabin's exit. By the time we got back to the van the sun was starting to rise so we piled in and headed back.

Glad to be back, my heart did a little happy dance until we entered the cabin only to find that it was empty. My heart quit dancing and dropped to the floor. The mats on the homemade wood floor were gone and the guns on the shelves were missing, otherwise it looked undisturbed.

"Mom, Dad," I called in a panic.

"Why is my phone on the table?" asked Sarah.

I turned. "What?" Her question was more than out of place. The expression on Bryce's face said he thought the same thing as we both walked towards her.

"My phone, it's even on. I know I didn't leave it out and I turned it off. I can't charge it and want the battery to last."

Bryce grabbed her by the shoulders. "Everyone is gone, our families, friends, even Cat, and you're worried about your phone?"

Her eyes shifted, not looking at either of us. "I'm not worried about the phone but why is it out? And everyone is gone – vanished."

Behind us, the bench creaked open. We spun on our heels and stared as a hand pushed the lid open then my father's head poked out.

"Dad," I ran towards him and wrapped my arms around his neck. "You're here, you're alive."

His face was soft as he embraced me. "We're all here."

One by one, we assisted everyone out. The chest doubled as a trap door to a basement they found by accident while searching for places to hide from the soldiers.

After everyone was out, my father's face hardened. "Where were you?"

All the adults wore the same stern expression. It was five to three. We stammered for a bit before Sarah finally burst out, "We explored and found out a whole bunch of stuff and a new boat, the zombies are all dead in piles all over the streets and we found a boy. Everyone gets all the excitement except for me so I wanted to go and my phone, it's laying on the table." She took a large breath after spitting out everything without one.

"Slow down. I didn't understand a word you said except the mention of your phone," said Katrina, hands folded across her chest as she eyeballed us.

"Your phone, where is it?" asked my father, suddenly more concerned about it than us.

She shoved it at him. He turned on the screen and gasped then went into a phone rant. "That's it. They used the GPS. That's how they target living people. Our phones haven't had reception or Wi-Fi but they have it. I guarantee they have it, they've blocked us but the GPS still sends a signal."

Yup, my father the smart-phone salesman. I thought the only benefit was getting the next best phone but I guess I was mistaken.

My mom cocked her head and glared at him then us. "How many of you have your phones?"

I felt as if it was something bad to have kept my phone and answered, "I do." I was ready to put out my wrists and let them cuff me and haul me to cell phone addiction jail.

"So do I," answered Bryce. I felt a bit better; at least I wouldn't be alone.

It turns out Sarah was the worst addict as she kept hers charged on the boat. Bryce and I stopped charging ours once we lost 4G and a connection.

My father narrowed his eyes and shook his head in dismay. "They're tracking GPS and are blocking all reception and Wi-Fi. Don't turn it off, let the battery run out."

My guilt disappeared, then I remembered the compass around my neck and the GPS inside it that tracked my whereabouts. "My compass," I said, nudging Bryce.

The corners of his mouth turned upward in a sly smile. "I turned the GPS off from my app after I found you. I figured if you're ever in trouble or lost I can turn it back on, but without phone capabilities that's impossible." Which made perfect sense since its battery hadn't died, yet when they found the van they didn't find us, even though the van belonged to a group they'd found in the woods.

My dad gave us a quizzical look. "What do you mean, 'compass'?"

"Well," I started, but wasn't going to tell him about how I brought it out of the dream. That was too weird, so I continued with a tiny white lie. "Bryce gave it to me. It isn't just a cool looking compass but has built in GPS."

"You have a compass?" Jack inquired.

"Yeah," then it hit me. It wasn't using GPS so could be used to help navigate home without using the boat's navigation and taking the chance of being found. "We can use it and it can't be tracked!"

Jack and my father nodded in agreement.

After a good reaming from our parents, Jack filled us in on what knowledge he had. The USS America was a new type of ship – a carrier that was smaller in size but made far more efficient use of its space. The lower deck carried amphibious vehicles manned by Marines. The boat was designed for landing planes, F-358s, and missions such as what we observed them doing in Morocco.

The ladder-thing we watched the soldiers use to enter and exit the flight deck was called a brow. I thought that was an odd name for it. The code 10-19 meant get back to base and the lower deck that carried the amphibious vehicles was called the well dock and the guns they carried were M-16s. The reason they used short bursts was because, as a semi-automatic, that's how the gun fired. I'd learned all types of military trivia from Jack. He was a wealth of knowledge.

Jack twisted a toothpick -- he'd found some in the cabin's kitchen -- in his mouth. "They're probably taking the uninfected back to a quarantine zone."

Katrina jumped into the conversation. "I think he's right and we should get onboard that carrier before it leaves." She smoothed her daughter's thick chestnut hair into a ponytail and wrapped a band around it.

"We don't know that," said Heather, her brows lowered in caution. "They may be using them for testing." As a doctor I saw her logic in that, after all she wanted to run tests and get blood samples on all of us, but I'd have thought she'd have wanted the sophisticated equipment of the US military to run those tests and the larger population sample.

"We've come this far on our own. I plan on keeping it that way, but no one is stopping anyone else from leaving," said my father, his eyes shifting from one person to the next.

153

"I'll go with her," said Jack, moving the toothpick to the other side of his mouth.

It was settled. My father would drive Jack, Katrina, Melissa, and Bryce to Casablanca and drop them within walking distance of the carrier then come back here and, once the ship left, we'd find Bennet and head back to the US.

When Katrina, as his mother, decided Bryce was going with her, my heart sank to the ground when he gave me sad I'm-sorry eyes, but didn't argue the decision. It was the equivalent of smashing my dropped heart and crunching it into the dirt with a heel. More than anything, I wanted to run to Bryce and beg him to stay then plead with Katrina *Don't make him go, tell him to stay.*

Regardless of the ways of my heart, I understood that was his family and he wanted to see them safe and protect them further if needed, but that didn't make it hurt less.

Chapter Twenty-One

Bryce...

As the van moved along the mountain road, Bryce saw the carrier was clearly still there. He wasn't sure about his mother's decision but had to go with his family. They were all he had left and he didn't want to lose them. As for the military, he trusted them. Growing up in a military town, he'd admired soldiers and had the most respect, but the world now was very different than it had been a few short weeks ago. He didn't know who to trust except the group he traveled with and he'd miss his zombie killing partner, Maddie. He didn't trust Bennet either, as he knew he lied. When they'd cleared the boat he'd noticed a picture in the master suite of a boy who looked a lot like Bennet with a black woman of light complexion and a white man. That matched Bennett's description of his parents. What didn't match was he said the boat wasn't his and they'd got there by plane. Bryce had no idea why he'd lie and brushed it off the night before, but now it seemed really important.

Bryce already missed his premonition sharing partner, Maddie. Her cute, dimpled smile, tilt of her head, and thick sun-bleached hair tied back in a ponytail that bobbed with each step were all his mind saw the further from her they got. They were going to explore the world together and find their way, now that wouldn't happen. His mother squeezed his hand.

The carrier was no longer in sight as they drove through the city. The bodies of the dead smelled even worse, like a combination of rotten egg farts and trash left sitting in the sun for too long. Some of the bodies were beginning to bloat. The sight was disgusting, he thought, and was glad his sister was too small to see out the windows.

His mother's face cringed as she looked away from the window. A few streets from the dock, Bill Whyte pulled the van over. "If I get any closer they'll see the van."

"It's been a journey," Jack said as he offered him his hand then slid the van door open.

Katrina smiled softly. "Thank you, and Maddie, for rescuing us. I'll never forget your kindness." Tears pooled in her eyes.

Holding his sister and telling her to bury her head, Bryce stepped out of the van. He took a few steps away from the van, then turned and walked back to the driver's seat and looked Bill square in the eye. "Let Maddie know I'll find her when it's safe."

Bill nodded confirmation and watched the small group walk toward the docks. He couldn't afford waiting and turned the van around and headed back.

"You miss him?" asked Heather.

"What?" I answered, my mind a million miles away as I remembered the premonition and Bryce's soft lips on mine. It had felt so real. The entire dream was real.

"Bryce, you miss him," she placed a hand on mine, resting in my lap.

I nodded. "Yeah, he's a friend, a good friend, and now I can't even contact him. No cell phones, radios, nothing," I answered, my eyes focused on a circular indent in the wooden floor.

"I think you both like each other as more than friends."

How perceptive! Was it that obvious? "I guess," I answered, pushing myself off the floor. I didn't feel like talking.

"My phone is officially dead," said Sarah with a sigh.

I chuckled. "When we get to the boat you can charge it, but remember to turn off the GPS," I warned in a voice mocking my father.

My mother narrowed her eyes at me then rolled them as she chose not to scold me.

"Right," Sarah answered, resting her head on my shoulder as we sat together on my mat. Cat walked between us, purring like a motor boat, sticking his butt in the air as we pet him. He walked back and forth, rolling his head on our hands.

The rumble of the van told me Dad returned. I stood and marched to the back window, hoping, wishing that Bryce would be with him, but he walked out of the shed alone.

I opened the door for him. "Is the carrier gone?"

"Yeah," he nodded, agreeing with his word. "Are you packed?"

"Yup." I pointed to our cart. Between nine people we'd pretty much wiped out the supplies from Spain and what was in the cabin.

Within the hour we'd loaded the van in preparation to leave, walking carefully around the zombie body part trail. The skin and muscles started falling away from their bones. My eyes went directly to the grotesque sight. I'd never seen anything like it. Taking a small branch, I jabbed it into the female's chest which split and fell to the sides around the puncture. The man's body was mushier when I pressed the end of the branch into it.

The lion hadn't returned since the day he scared me and Bryce. I hadn't seen any animals; like they were hiding. The zombies gone, I expected them to return but they hadn't. *Was it the smell? Were their rotten bodies somehow affecting the environment?* My thoughts brought me full circle to the few animal sightings we'd had and the idea that they were trying to warn or protect us.

I took one last look at my home for the past several days, when a vehicle crunching the dirt road made my heart stop cold in my chest, my breath caught in my throat and I stumbled backwards.

My dad's voice interrupted my thoughts, "Hurry, Maddie!"

I blinked, then rushed toward him, taking one last glance around, I realized I'd zoned out. The house was empty and my dad held the lid of the bench up, everybody was already downstairs in the basement. As he closed the lid I heard a car door close outside.

Chapter Twenty-Two

Except for the light from a single flashlight, the downstairs was dark. The floor was concrete and the walls were unfinished. Squinting my eyes in the darkness, I spotted a bed in the corner and a large cabinet along with a long wooden table and a couple wood chairs. They looked homemade. Large jugs were stacked at the end of the wall.

Dust and something else mingled in the air, giving it an odor of something old like walking into a house that had been vacant for years. It was the perfect place for a monster or zombie to jump out of a shadowy corner like in a horror movie. Sarah grabbed my arm and planted herself next to me. My body shuddered as I grabbed onto her arm and we held tight to one another, our bodies so close I felt her heart beating against me.

We clung to each other as footsteps pounded the wooden floor above our heads. My parents stood only a few feet away, not far from the ladder that brought us down to the musty blackness. More footsteps pounded the floor of varying weights based on the hardness of their footsteps. One set was heavy, another much lighter, another one was panicky and ran around. A weightier step moved closer to the bench.

I wanted to sink into the darkness of the room. My dad cut the flashlight off and stepped backwards. He and my mom backed against the wall and slid closer to me. The chest lid opened and light streamed down into the room, surrounding the ladder and splashing sunbeams across the floor.

"Maddie," called a deep male voice – Bryce.

Sarah and I jumped into the air and rushed toward the ladder. I tripped over my father's feet and fell into the light beams beneath the ladder, the concrete floor rough against my palms and I knew I'd have fresh cuts and scrapes.

"Ouch!" grumbled my father.

"Are you Ok?" asked Sarah as she lowered herself, resting her knees on the floor.

"Sorry Dad. I'm alright," I replied as the ladder rattled and the view of Bryce's jeaned butt was above my head. *Not a bad view,* I thought.

Bryce stepped onto the concrete and knelt down, taking my hand. Jack's face appeared at the opening. "Was a no go. Ship already set sail."

Bryce and I stepped aside as everyone went back upstairs. He held my hands as we waited and whispered in my ear. "I'm glad it was gone. I didn't want to leave; to leave you."

His warm breath against my face sent tingles coursing over my body and his hands strong and firm around mine. I was glad too; I didn't want him to leave. We had a connection that was beyond human explanation.

By the time we got upstairs, my dad and Jack were deep in conversation while Melissa was happy to see Cat and he purred as she picked him up. His feet dangled beneath her lower arm but it didn't bother him, instead he rubbed his head against her chest. We had an otherworldly connection to him as well, something I couldn't explain. It was like the three of us had to stay together.

"When we got to the dock the boat was already several miles off shore so we jacked a car and came back," said Bryce, shoving his hands in his front pockets.

Jack jumped in, "It's heading straight west, probably to Norfolk, Virginia."

My dad cupped his chin in thought. We stood silent as each of us considered his words, then Bryce spoke, "I think maybe we should follow it, see where it's going and what they're doing with those people."

"I need a lab," said Heather, her voice straight and serious. "Whatever caused the disease, we don't want it to come back or evolve into something worse. I don't want to turn into a flesh-eater."

What was worse than most of the human population of the world becoming flesh-eating deaders? Stupid question, the entire population would be worse.

Out of the blue, Katrina mumbled something then her eyes widened into starships. "Wetland Environment and Conservation," she said it again, then added, "WEAC. We need to get back to the states."

Bryce's face lit up, "The company dad's company contracted with. Mom, do you think they have something to do with this?"

She shrugged. "Maybe. I don't know. He was overseeing an environmental testing that involved mosquitoes. Something must have gone wrong, why else would he choose it as his last words? We need to find out."

The room was again silent, then my mother, who rested on a homemade wooden chair, stood. "We need to do both. Split up. Jack can follow the carrier and take a couple of us with him. Katrina," her gaze shifted to Bryce's mom, "you, me, Melissa, Bill, and Heather will go back to the states and figure this out."

She didn't mention me going with her. *Does that mean I have permission to go with Jack, or choose? Was she beginning to see me as more than her little girl in this dangerous new world?* "What about me and Sarah and Bryce?"

She smiled, filled with warmth contradicted by her lowered brows. "You are all nearing adulthood and I think should decide for yourselves."

Katrina's and my father's eyes narrowed as they stared at her in anger and surprise. "Honey, they're still children," my father stated. Katrina nodded her head in agreement.

"Yes, and they have proved they can survive in this world. They are only children in biological age and Bryce is almost eighteen. Mentally, they are adults and have acted like adults." She gave him the don't-argue-with-me stare.

Sarah's eyes blazed at me then shifted to Bryce. Our eyes met and spoke silently. "I'm going to the States. I want to know what caused this thing and I hold part of the answer inside me."

Sarah spoke next as she took a couple steps forward, "I'm going to the states too, with Maddie. I was bitten yet never got sick. I want to know why and help."

My parents' eyes filled with love and beamed pride with our *adult* decisions.

Bryce's gaze bore into mine and I knew his decision even before he spoke it. "I'm going with Jack. I'll be more help to him."

Katrina closed her eyes and sniffled. A single tear dripped over her cheek bone and rolled down her face. She only nodded. Her boy was nearly a man. I'd miss him too and wish for his safe return, but I respected his decision and so did Katrina. She walked up to her son, wrapped her arms around him and whispered something in his ear.

Chapter Twenty-Three

We reached the dock after making a pit stop for supplies. We'd pretty much wiped out the supplies and food we picked up in Spain and what was left in the cabin. When we reached the boat, it looked even larger during the day. Bennet didn't greet us, not right away. I set my bags of groceries on the table when he entered the room.

His choice of clothing was better, at least his blue polo matched his gray sweatpants, but the sliders still looked out of place, at least on him with his oddball shaped toes. He half-smiled and shifted nervously when I introduced him to everyone. He was a strange bird. I left everyone to get acquainted.

Jack climbed onto a sailboat, larger than Earnest Earl. It was also newer and more stream-lined, like it was built for speed. I watched from the dock as the two of them searched the boat.

Katrina and Melissa joined me after several minutes. Bryce and Jack exited the boat's cabin. Jack stayed onboard but Bryce joined us on the dock. "What do you think?"

"Nice," I answered. Everything was nicer when you had your choice and didn't need money. I thought of the trinkets I stole in Spain, from the zombies, that were still in my pocket.

Bryce picked up his chubby-cheeked, golden-haired sister. He twirled her above him and she giggled. The motor of Jack and Bryce's stolen boat caught and purred.

A warm hand curled around mine. "Thank you, for everything. Saving us in Italy and knowing what to do when the zombies attacked us. You saved Melissa's life."

It was the right thing, the only thing to do. I wasn't a heroine, just a fifteen-year-old girl surviving in a ruthless world that took no prisoners. My lips tugged upwards at the corners. "They'll be alright, you know." Her green eyes like shiny jade stones watched Bryce and Melissa.

She nodded. "And so will we. I'm glad you're coming with us."

I didn't expect that from her, but squeezed her hand in response as confirmation. Melissa scurried back to her mom and waved at Bryce as they strolled toward the boat. My dad fired the engine that was even quieter than the other boat.

The ash clouds were finally clearing and the sun beamed on our heads as Bryce walked towards me. He took my hands in his. "I'm going to miss you, Zombie Girl."

I gave him a sideways smile as my hands melted inside his like streusel glaze on cinnamon rolls. "I might miss you too." I sighed.

"We'll find each other." He lifted a hand and brushed it against my chest, lifting the compass. The touch of his skin against mine lingered.

I smiled and used my empty hand to grab onto a belt loop of his jeans. It felt natural to stand there with him, our bodies so near each other. He took a step closer and brushed a stray hair behind my ear, his mouth dangerously close to mine. The heat from his breath rushed across my face as he lowered his head. His mouth parted and his soft lips touched mine, sending tingles through my body.

Electricity raced through me as his tongue entered my mouth. Instinctively, my tongue met his and they swirled together. The world around us disappeared and it was only us in what was my first actual kiss from a boy.

"Take care of them," he whispered as he pulled away, our hands still clutched together until it was just our fingers and then the tips.

My hand dropped to my side. "I will."

"Time to go, Maddie," hollered my mom from the deck. She winked, her lips pulled upwards in a smile. I felt my face go flush. *Did she see us? How long had she stood there?*

I scurried towards the boat and climbed on. As our boat pulled out, I watched Bryce and Jack until they were a tiny dot on the horizon. We were heading to Jacksonville, Florida and they were heading to Norfolk, Virginia or where ever the USS America was going.

We snatched four sets of long-range walkie-talkies and Bryce jacked another compass and set of binoculars. Their boat a blip on the watery horizon, I strolled inside. Everyone was in the cabin, mingling, except my dad. He was driving the boat and probably fiddling with all the cool gadgets on the bridge. Bennet shifted uneasily and contorted his lips as he watched everyone, then his eyes enlarged into footballs staring at something behind me.

One by one, everyone stopped talking and turned, staring wide-eyed at something or someone behind me. I heard two sets of footsteps behind me and instinctively whipped my head around.

Zombie Girl 2 Infection

About the Author

Elle Klass is the author of mystery, suspense, and contemporary fiction. Her works include *As Snow Falls, Eye of the Storm Eilida's Tragedy,* and the *Baby Girl* series. Her work *Eye of the Storm* Eilida's *Tragedy* is a Reader's Favorite Fiction-Paranormal Finalist in the 2015 Reader's Favorite Awards. *Baby Girl Box Set* received Official Honors in Young Adult through New Apple Indie Ebook Awards. She is a night-owl where her imagination feeds off shadows, and creaks in the attic. Visit her website at https://elleklass.weebly.com.